THE BIG OLE LEGEND

An American Icon with Minnesota Roots

AMP-Squared Books
A Division of AMP2, LLC
www.ampsquared.com

© 2014 by AMP-Squared Books. All Rights Reserved: No portion may be used or reproduced without written permission.

First Edition, August 2014
Printed in the United States of America

Cover Image Photography/Design: Kerry Olson

AMP-Squared Books - A Division of AMP2, LLC
316 N. Nokomis Street, Ste. #1, Alexandria MN 56308
(320)763-3742
Email: books@ampsquared.com
www.ampsquared.com

Editor: Julie Zuehlke
Art Director: Kerry Olson
Senior Graphic Designer: Lynn Barton
Contributing Writer and Editor: Marjorie Van Gorp
Marketing and Financial Coordinator: Bryan Boutain

ISBN: 978-0-9897926-0-8

The information contained in this book constitutes a bio-simulography of an American historic and cultural icon with Minnesota roots in Alexandria. It is a work of fiction with characters created by the authors. Names, places and incidents are interlaced with actual events and people. Any reference or resemblance to actual persons, living or deceased, is coincidental.

ON THE COVER:

Construction of the Big Ole statue began in 1964 for the
New York World's Fair representing the State of Minnesota.
The statue took its permanent place as a proud representative
of American heritage and Scandinavian pride
in Alexandria, Minnesota,
arriving on December 21, 1965.

Photo and Illustration Credits

P. iii,124: © Bill Cotter. Big Ole and globe at the 1965 World's Fair in New York. http://www.worldsfairphotos.com.

P. 12, 44, 56, 76, 106, 114, 116, 130: Pencil illustrations by Mike Christiansen. www.flightadv.com.

P. 13 : Marjorie Van Gorp personal archives, trunk belonged to her uncle, Johan Magnus Akesson, who came to North America in the early 1890s.

P. 18 : Marjorie Van Gorp personal archives, passenger ship SS Parisian (Allan Line) was a common conveyance for Europeans emigrating to North America from the 1880s through the 1930s.

P. 22 : Wall mural of the Vikings route by sea. Painting by Christopher Andersen, located in the Runestone Museum in Alexandria, Minnesota.

P. 50, 90, 98, 124: Photos by Kerry Olson.

P. 34 and 128 : Marjorie Van Gorp personal archives, photo of her maternal grandmother, Minnie Fischer, circa 1895.

P. 74 : Railroad men working on the Great Northern Railway, from the collection of Douglas County Historical Society.

P. 20, 22, 24, 30, 32, 36, 60, 66, 68, 70, 84, 94, 96 : Stock photo images from www.shutterstock.com.

P. 32, 46, 78, 86, 88 : Stock photo images and vector artwork from www.ingimage.com.

P. 102 : Johnson's Minnesota and Dakota map, by Johnson and Ward circa 1864.

P. 104 : Fort Alexandria circa 1862. Painting by Ada Johnson, located in the Runestone Museum in Alexandria, Minnesota.

THE BIG OLE LEGEND

This book belongs to:

Written by Marjorie Van Gorp
Edited and Co-Authored by Julie Zuehlke
Art Direction and Design by Kerry Olson
Illustrator: Mike Christiansen

AMP-Squared Books
Alexandria, Minnesota

ACKNOWLEGMENTS

Definitive Woman Magazine
Letters from Big Ole's Mother first appeared as a five-part series from Winter 2009 through Winter 2010-11.

Douglas County Historical Society

Runestone Museum

Sentinel Printing Co.

Reviewers
Erica Fulghum
Diane and Dale Swanson

DEDICATION

Thank you to the hundreds of volunteers, businesses and organizations of Alexandria who brought Big Ole to life and continue to maintain the Big Ole Statue as a cultural icon, public art, and visitor attraction commemorating the rich history, heritage and traditions that boost community spirit.

TABLE OF CONTENTS

INTRODUCTION IX

FACTIDS 10, 38, 80, 107, 122

CHAPTER 1 – *Letters from Big Ole's Mother*
Their Journey Begins 16
Meeting Thorvald 20
A Comfort of Home 24

CHAPTER 2 – *Letters from Big Ole's Mother*
Dining Aboard Ship 30
Slow Going on Land 34

CHAPTER 3 – *Letters from Big Ole's Mother*
Bound to the Land 42
Smooth Sailing 48

CHAPTER 4 – *Letters from Big Ole's Mother*
Making New Friends 54
On the Move Again 58

CHAPTER 5 – *Letters from Big Ole's Mother*
On American Soil 64
Wrong Train 68
A Work Stop 72
A Hero Again 76

CHAPTER 6 – *Letters from Big Ole's Mother*
Catching Up 84
Enjoying the Scenery 88

CHAPTER 7 – *Letters from Big Ole's Mother*
Ole's River Plunge 94
Brown Beans and a Gold Keepsake 98
New Home at Last 102

CHAPTER 8 – *Journal and Letter Excerpts*
Growing up, Becoming a Leader, Marriage, Death 113-121

WORLD'S FAIR DEBUT of Big Old Statue/Timeline 124
OTHER MINNESOTA STATUES 127
ABOUT MEKTILD 128
ABOUT THE AUTHORS 130
ORDERING INFORMATION 132

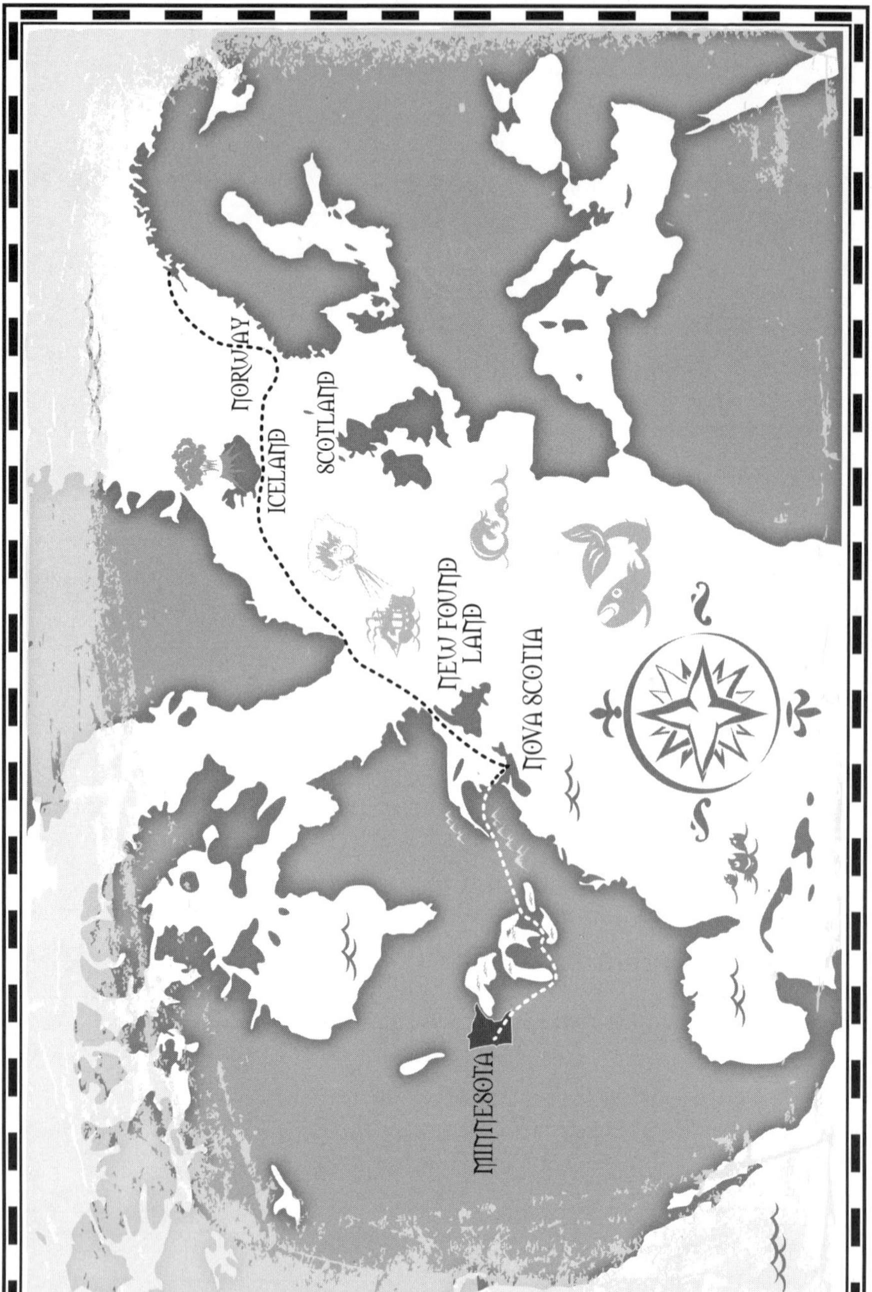
NORWAY
ICELAND
SCOTLAND
NEW FOUND LAND
NOVA SCOTIA
MINNESOTA

INTRODUCTION

Big Ole has come to symbolize the ruggedness
of the explorers and settlers, the brave men and women,
who founded America.

This account of Big Ole offers a glimpse
into an iconic hero's life
from his childhood in northern Europe
and proud Scandinavian peoples
through his journey to America
where his legendary life in began in Minnesota.

Map at left shows the Scandinavian lands to the east and the Atlantic Ocean that Mektild and her son, Big Ole, crossed westward to make a new home in Minnesota, United States, North America.

Twelve "Factids" about Big Ole

(NOTE: A "factid" represents a FACtual TIDbit about a person, place, or thing which offers further interesting detail that might not be contained in the main body of a written work.)

– Factid #1 –
Big Ole's real statue resides in Alexandria, Minnesota.

– Factid #2 –
He was a Scandinavian immigrant.

– Factid #3 –
Big Ole was 6-foot-3-inches tall. His robust nature, muscular build, and congenial personality made him seem larger than life.

– Factid #4 –
His ancestors were real Vikings.

– Factid #5 –
He was a skilled horseman and teamster who loved the outdoors. He was an avid hunter and fisherman.

– Factid #6 –
Big Ole's statue depicts wings on the helmet as a modern interpretation of traditional Viking garb. Actual Viking helmets had neither horns nor wings.

– Factid #7 –
His skills included carpentry, woodworking and metalworking.

– Factid #8 –
Big Ole's friends included high-level state officials, politicians and dignitaries as well as railroad magnates and frontier developers.

– Factid #9 –
While Big Ole lived around the same time as the famed Paul Bunyan, the two were never friends as is sometimes rumored in the press. Besides, Paul Bunyan is not really a person.

– Factid #10 –
He was not a contemporary of the other famed Minnesota icon, Jolly Green Giant, whose statue stands in Blue Earth, Minnesota. The vegetable man is not really a person either.

– Factid #11 –
Big Ole's statue is one of the most photographed Viking images in the country.

– Factid #12 –
Big Ole was born on July 4, 1867 on a Scandinavian island.

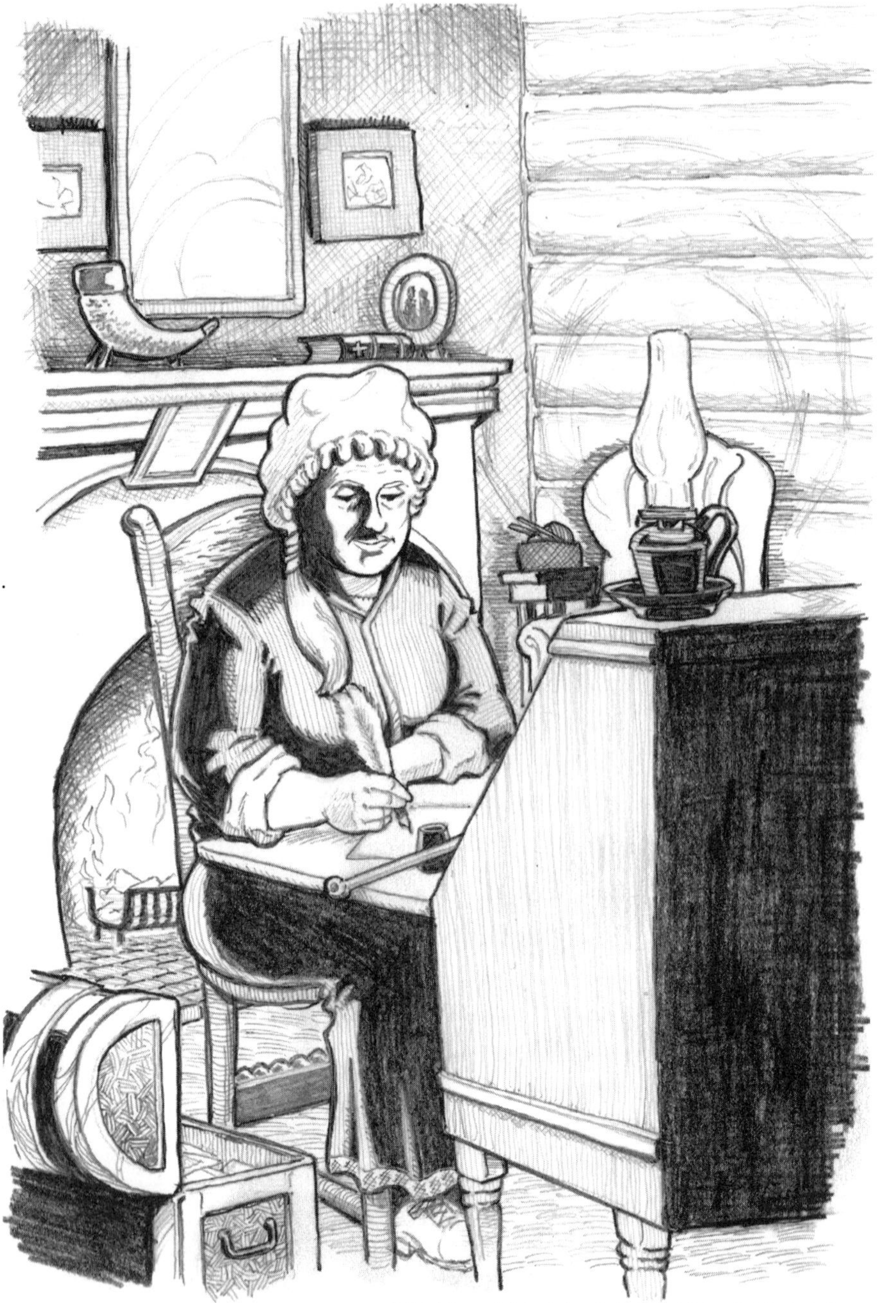

ᛗᛖᚱᚲᛏᛁᛚᛞ ᚹᚨᛚᛞᛁᛊ ᚷᚢᛚᛞ

Letters From Big Ole's Mother

The letters are excerpts and anecdotes pieced together from bundles found in an old trunk many years after they were written by Mektild Valdis Guld.

About The Letters

The Letters from Big Ole's Mother were featured as a series of five stories in *Definitive Woman Magazine* in Winter 2009-10, Spring 2010, Summer 2010, Fall 2010, and Winter 2010-11.

They tell the story of Mektild Valdis Guld who brought her young son across the North Atlantic into Canada and eventually to America settling in west central Minnesota.

Mektild was a fierce guardian of his safety while allowing him freedom to explore and learn. She was a wise and accomplished woman who instilled in her son the values of learning and the responsibilities of being a good man.

Their journey was arduous, sometimes even hazardous and frightening. Along the way, she wrote letters to relatives in Scandinavia recounting their adventures into a new life.

Letters from Big Ole's Mother

CHAPTER ONE

The Journey Begins

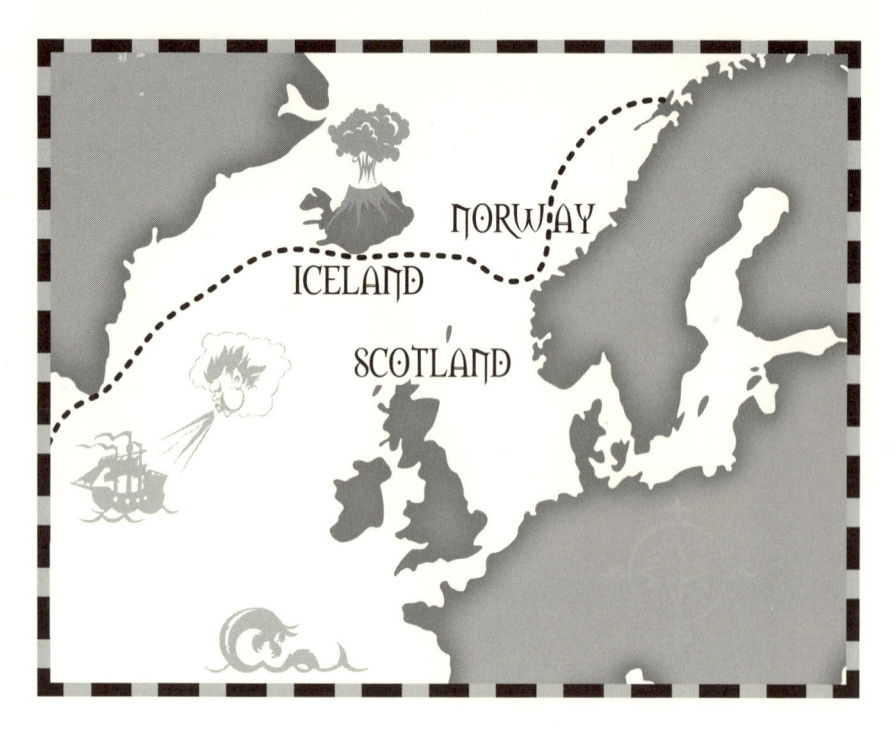

My Dearest Sister Bornhild,

How sad for Ole and I to embark on a journey that will take us so far away from you and the rest of our dear family, not knowing when, or if, we will ever see you again. And how exciting at the same time to think of building a new life in a new land. That helps diminish the sadness a bit. and knowing that we will be greeted by other family members upon our arrival makes it seem less dangerous.

The trip over the vast waters from Norden to our first landing in North America was long and arduous. The voyage began on a small freighter from Barents Bay and out into the sea where we headed southward toward the North Sea.

Even Ole, who isn't quite fully schooled in geography yet, could see the oddity of going toward something named "north" by heading south.

S. S. Parisian. (Allan Line.)

Perhaps that one little question is enough to make me believe there might be something inside his head besides childish whimsy and foolishness!

 I was a little concerned about Ole on the first leg of our trip. He brooded a lot and spent most of his time sitting on the deck staring at the water or tinkering with his Runic kewbs. When we were waiting to board our ocean-going vessel after we left the freighter, he became more social.

 We boarded the ocean liner, the Scanda Huvyan, in Bergen and almost immediately, Ole wandered off to listen to a salty looking character telling stories to other boys. The storyteller was a ship's mate respected by the crew and his name was Thorvald. He claimed to have been orphaned when he was about Ole's age and brought up by a deck crew on a freighter.

Your Loving Sister, Mektild

Meeting Thorvald

Dearest Bornhild,

I must tell you more about Ole's new friend. Thorvald is a seasoned sailor. In his thirties, he had seen every curve of the earth and knows just about everything anyone needs to know about sailing and adventure. He got Ole interested in geography, sailing, and growing up.

The tales he told of adventure and misadventure mesmerized Ole and soon he was following Thorvald around like a pet reindeer. He took a liking to Ole and soon they developed a strong bond. I became concerned about his friendship until I saw that Ole took an interest in the bigger world around him.

Never before had Ole seemed aware of the rising and falling of the tides or the different looks to the setting sun or navigating by the stars. He suddenly wanted to learn everything and Thorvald became his mentor. He taught Ole important life lessons beyond what he'd learned in the neighborhood schooling groups back home.

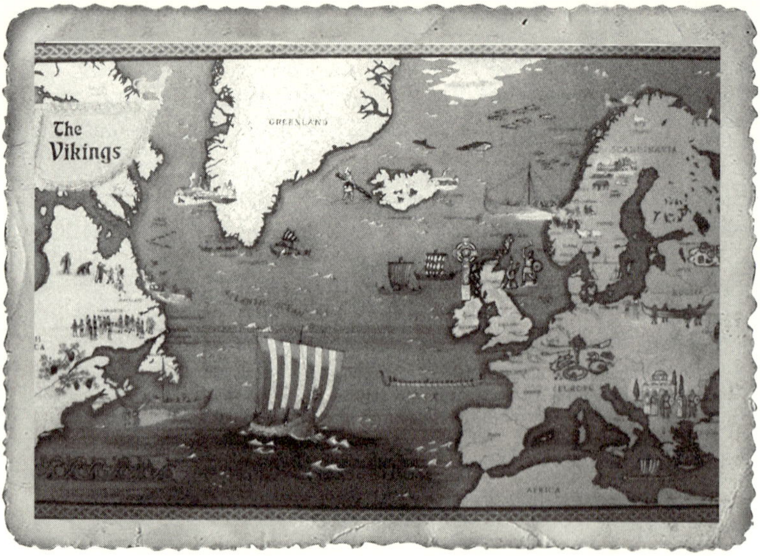
The Vikings
GREENLAND
SCANDINAVIA
EUROPE
AFRICA

I was greatly pleased that Ole took such a great step toward becoming a responsible man, even if it was under the tutelage of this crusty older sailor. Thorvald seems trustworthy and solid.

Ole misses his father, though I certainly do not. I recognize the fierce Viking traits that will surely rise up in him someday. It's hard to ignore what must be embittered and embattled childhood memories he carries in his young head. I hope the spirited strength of his ancestors, including mine, will win out and serve him well in his future.

Hoping this letter finds you in good stead, I remain,

Your loving sister, Mektild

A Comfort of Home

Dearest Sister,

Bornhild, you will never believe what happened during the first week aboard the Scanda Huvyan. The captain asked if any of us would like to help make flatbread with the ship's cook! I think this is a tradition involving passengers, although I can't say for sure, this being my first ocean voyage. Anyway, you know me and my flatbread skills and love for baking so I was quick to volunteer to help!

I went to find Ole by looking for Thorvald. I knew Ole wouldn't be far from his mentor and sure enough, they were both in the galley! I was surprised to see that Thorvald was teaching Ole how to make flatbread dough just like we did it in Norden. It was even more surprising that he was enjoying the work! Can you imagine that Ole would be so cheerful about doing that chore?
Yet there he was, helping to make the potato flatbread! Thorvald seems to be having a good influence on your rambunctious nephew.

Many men of the crew were helping, too. Some were peeling potatoes they had brought up from

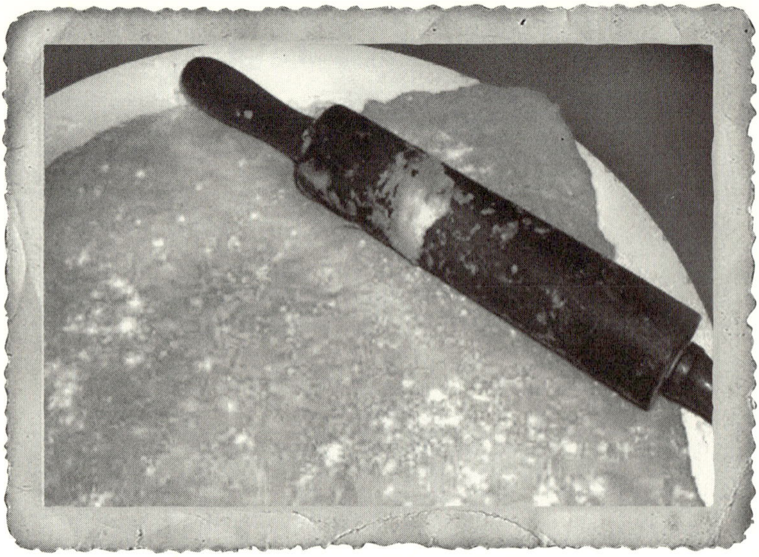

the hold. Some were boiling and mashing them. Those men had the technique perfect, efficiently making the dough just like the men back home who would do the harder work of preparing the dough for the women to roll out. They knew to add a fistful of salt and just enough water to make the dough easy to work.

   Women always do the best job of the rolling out and the baking. Perhaps that's why the captain recruited volunteers from the passengers knowing the results would be the best. One older lady passenger was really excellent at it. She rolled that dough as thin as a bed sheet before she unfurled it on the oven bottom. When it was ready to come out of the oven, she rushed the warm circle of nostalgic goodness for the next woman to lay it flat and dust off with a whiskbroom. That woman was an expert at the gentle folding technique. She treated it like a fine tablecloth.

   The whole process made me feel more at home and less afraid of our journey and what was to come in our new land.

Your loving sister, Mektild

Letters from Big Ole's Mother

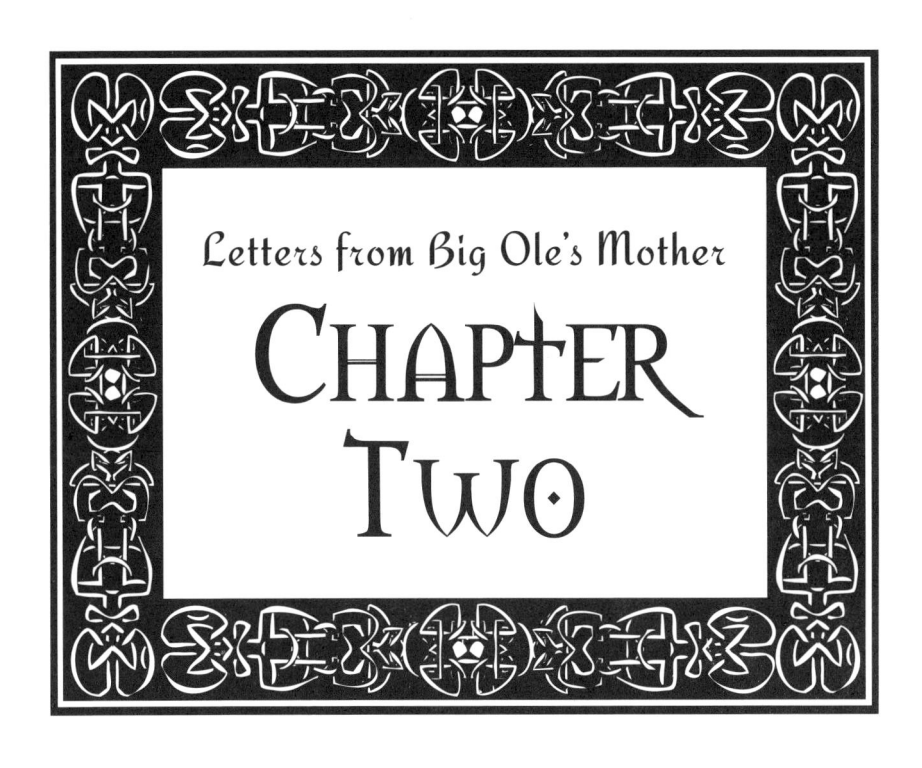

Chapter Two

Dining Aboard Ship

Dearest Sister,

My last letter spoke about making flatbread aboard ship. Let me tell you about the mainstay of our diet while sailing on the open water and far from pantries, root cellars, and larders.

Our staples consisted of dried fruits and dried cod. We had salted venison, cheese brought from our own dairies and plenty of flour for making bread. Fancy pastries and desserts were not an every day occurrence. The flatbread we made was the only "fresh" food. We eagerly awaited landing in the Shetlands so we could get some fresh fruit and some fresh grains from the Faeroes.

Sadly, that didn't happen because of the fog. We couldn't make land in the Shetlands and were never even close enough to get a glimpse of the fields of the Faeroes. Even Greenland was one big clump of inedible frozen tundra so we had to bypass that, too.

When we came to port in Iceland, we had good weather so could finally disembark for a while. That gave us the opportunity to see at last about procuring some local food.

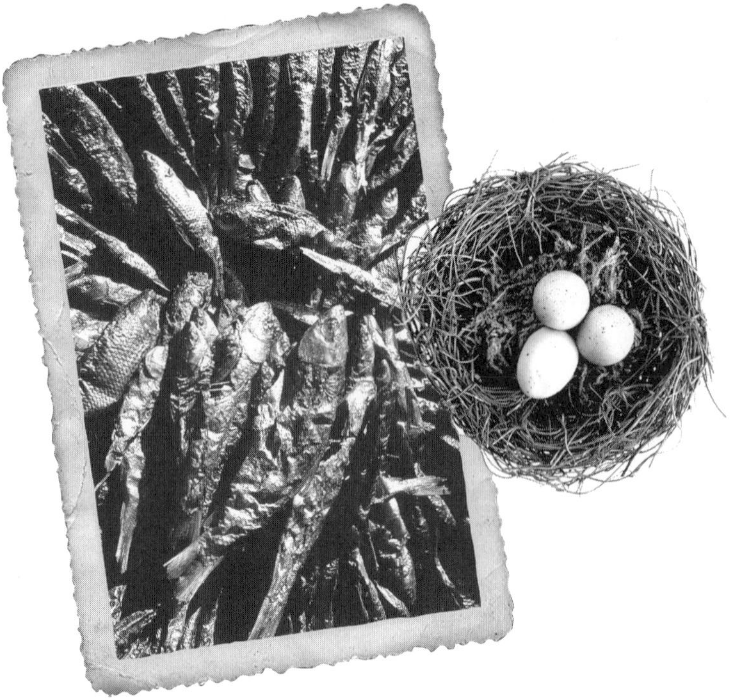

Thorvald had connections so he and Ole set about gathering fresh local eggs. The captain knew a farmer near the landing docks who traded fresh meat for some of our homemade Norden cheese.

That last stop before hitting the shores of North America was a welcome one and gave us a renewed spirit of excitement as we slogged on through the Atlantic Ocean.

When we finally landed in Nova Scotia, we had many more sources for replenishing our food supply to continue our journey.

We're spending some layover time here in Nova Scotia and thankfully, we have Uncle Gustav here who assured me that we would not be allowed to starve. It's also a blessing that he works for the railroad and helped us secure our passage to the edge of the new frontier via rail.

When the railroad tracks run out, we will arrange for different overland transport providing us another new adventure as we make our way toward the middle of this grand, huge continent.

Your loving sister, Mektild

Slow-Going On Land

My Dearest Sister Gornhild,

How sad for Ole and I to embark on a journey that will take us so far away from you and the rest of our dear family, not knowing when, or if, we will ever see you again. And how exciting at the same time to think of building a new life in a new land. That helps diminish the sadness some and knowing that we will be greeted by other family members makes it seem less dangerous.

The trip over the vast waters from Norden to our first landing in North America was long and arduous. The voyage began on a small freighter from Barents Bay and out into the sea where we headed southward to the North Sea.

Even Ole, who isn't quite fully schooled in geography yet, could see the oddity of heading south to get to the open waters of the North Sea. Perhaps that one little question is enough to make me believe there might be something inside his head besides childish whimsy and foolishness!

Dearest Bornhild,

    Thank you for getting word to me that you share my messages with family, friends and neighbors. It gives me comfort to know so many people feel like they are with us.

    We are still citybound on the east coast of North America and our accommodations are adequate. There are plenty of things to do such as helping with chores in exchange for a reduced fee on room and board.

    Uncle Gustav received word from cousins Wilhelm and Aleksander that they've pushed further westward than anticipated into a place called Minnesota. I'm told the western prairies and lakes are an unending surprise. We are headed into a wilderness where dangers from native peoples exist and the newly established government is rebuilding from its War Between the States. The rest of our journey will be slow going overland. Not all of it is arranged as yet because of new developments almost on a weekly basis. We must be prepared to be patient and strong.

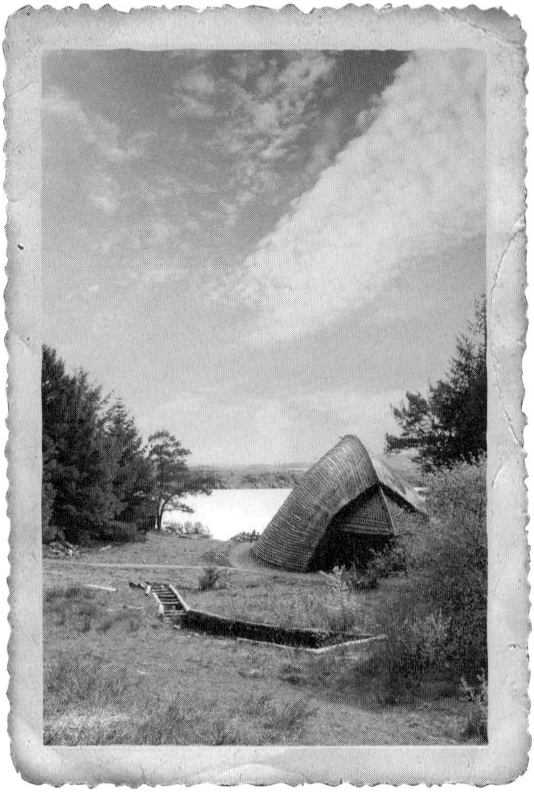

We've heard via our cousins and their companions that many folks are building encampments and home sites throughout this new territory that contain Nordenic and Scandian havens for those coming from the old country.

It's a grand new life we'll have, little Ole and me. I must soon stop calling him "little." I know one day he'll become "Big Ole." I will work hard to ensure he earns and deserves the respect that will pay homage to our heritage.

Your intrepid adventurer, Mektild

Twelve More "Factids" about Big Ole

– Factid #13 –
Big Ole had his early, formal education in the old country. He was self-taught and mentored for the remainder of his schooling.

– Factid #14 –
He learned sewing skills from his mother and aunt when he was a youngster, then helped make his own clothes through adulthood.

– Factid #15 –
Big Ole was an avid reader of newspapers and books and could learn other languages easily.

– Factid #16 –
He was a baseball fan.

– Factid #17 –
He loved to go fishing and he loved to eat fish.

– Factid #18 –
Big Ole played several musical instruments and was mostly self-taught.

– Factid #19 –
His mother raised him without his father.

– Factid #21 –
*His father had disappeared when
Big Ole was just 5 years old.*

– Factid #22 –
He knew how to card wool and spin it into yarn.

– Factid #23 –
*By the time he was 9 years old, back in his native land,
he was a good cook and knew how to bake bread,
pastries and other desserts.*

– Factid #24 –
*Big Ole's eyes were each a different color.
One was dark blue, almost indigo,
and the other a deep violet-brown.*

– Factid #25 –
His middle name is Torger.

Letters from Big Ole's Mother

Chapter Three

Bound to the Land

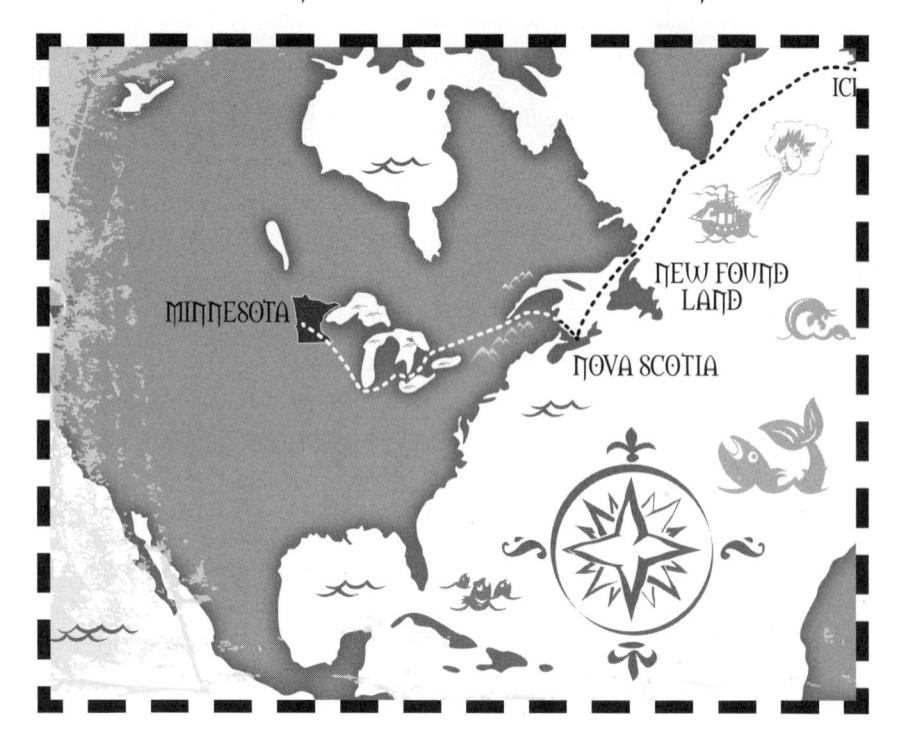

Dearest Sister,

We are still waiting to begin our overland journey from these North American shores in Nova Scotia so it's a good time to catch up with news I've not told you. I keep a journal and will relate some of those items to you here.

I miss the springtime landscape and the promise that is summer in the homeland. We spent the best part of the season on the water and here still on the coast of North America, summer is slow to emerge.

Uncle Gustav sure knew what he was saying when he told us about all the new adventures we'd experience. So much has already happened to us and it's been exciting traveling with little Ole and watching him grow and learn new things. He's becoming so much like his father it frightens me. Luckily so far, with Ole things seem to end in a good way.

I didn't get to tell you in my last letter about the trouble we had boarding the Scanda Huvyan. You can guess that "trouble" was because of Ole. I think the first letter "T" in his middle name stands for trouble instead of Torger.

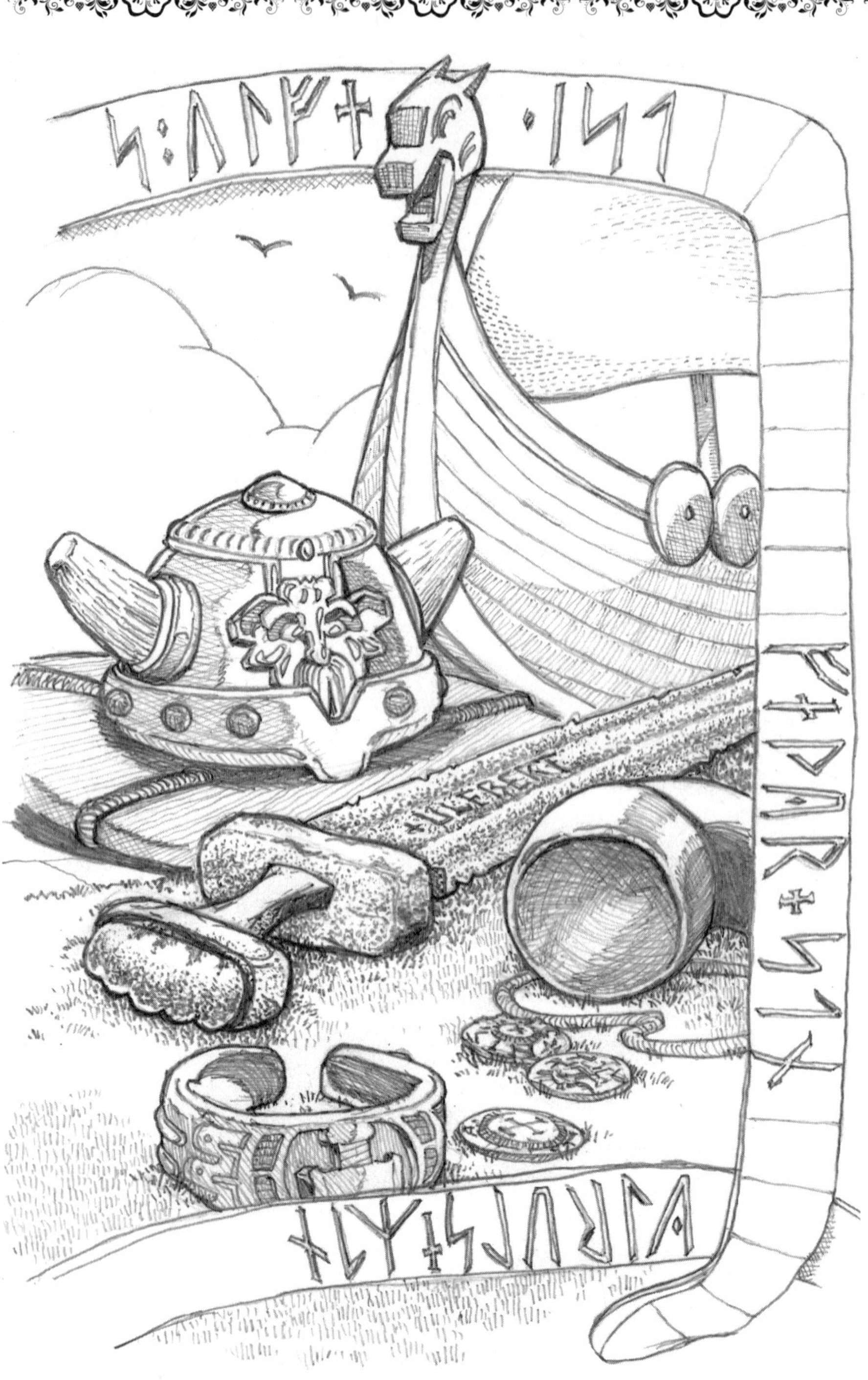

With his big size and burly features, he's looking like a young Eric the Red. The family line is even more evident because of his new scraggly beard beginning to poke through. He's looking scruffy from all the travel and finding every opportunity to roughhouse and get dirty.

Because of his appearance and the fact that he carries his game spear all the time, he caught the attention of some dockside constables. A couple of the officials whisked him aside and questioned him.

They perhaps thought him to be a criminal because he appeared to be brandishing a weapon. They weren't going to let him board with his prized souvenir spear.

He had two choices: he could place the spear in the hold during the voyage or he could leave it behind with the officials in Bergen.

True to the ways of his father, Ole was not about to give in without a negotiation. His argument was,

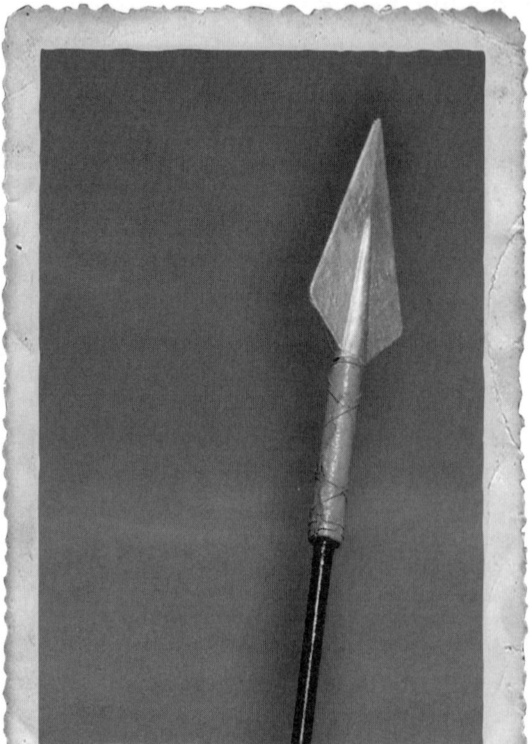

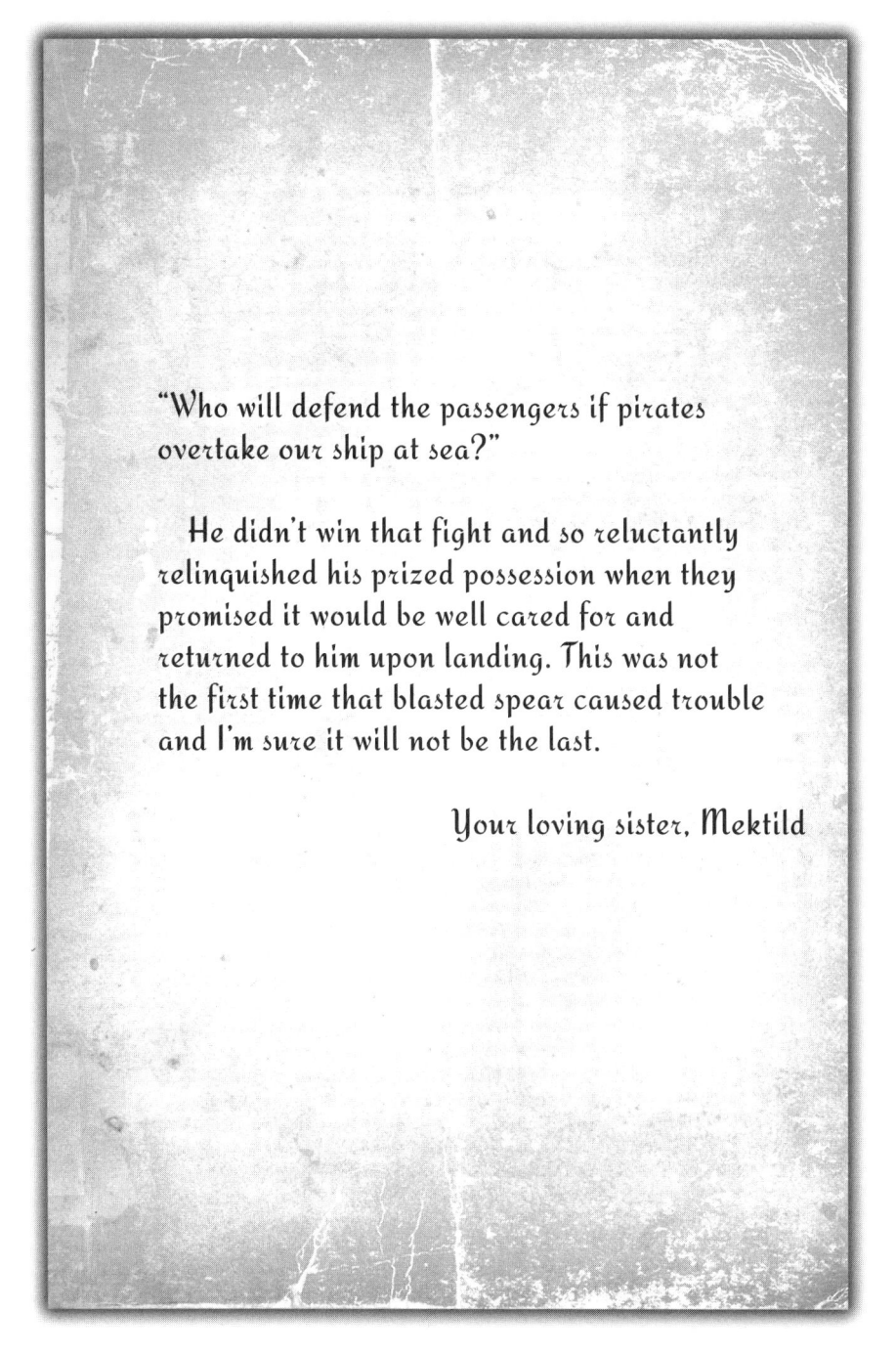

"Who will defend the passengers if pirates overtake our ship at sea?"

He didn't win that fight and so reluctantly relinquished his prized possession when they promised it would be well cared for and returned to him upon landing. This was not the first time that blasted spear caused trouble and I'm sure it will not be the last.

Your loving sister, Mektild

Smooth Sailing

Dearest Bornhild,

Our sea crossing had progressed without disastrous incident, no pirates as Ole had secretly hoped. The passengers were happy to set foot safely on land at Halifax. You cannot imagine the chaos when all those weary people scrambled for their traveling trunks and sea chests.

Ole and I were grateful that Uncle Gustav had advised us to have everything except our travel needs shipped ahead and straight through to our final destination across the continent. There was plenty of pandemonium with everyone pushing and shoving to find their belongings.

Nothing could compare to the panic that engulfed Ole when the deck hands couldn't find his spear. He was fit to be tied to the riggin' and he was spittin' mad! He had earned the ownership right to that family spear as the sixth generation javelin champion in the Norden games. Without that spear, he would never feel comfortable.

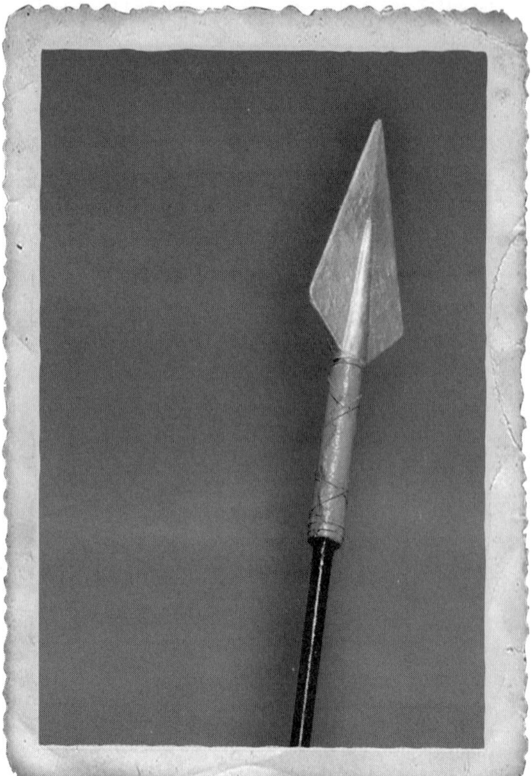

At the peak of his panic, when everyone else had left the ship, Thorvald appeared on deck brandishing Ole's spear! He hadn't trusted some of the ship's crew to safeguard it so he had secretly stashed it away in a safe place known only to him. He'd not told anyone, including Ole, so its whereabouts wouldn't accidentally slip out. And ship's policy about weapons was strict so it couldn't be returned to Ole until all other passengers had disembarked.

And so it was that Ole was reunited with his beloved spear bringing him joy on our first day on solid ground since leaving the homeland.

                  Fond thoughts and love to all, Mektild

Letters from Big Ole's Mother

CHAPTER FOUR

Making New Friends

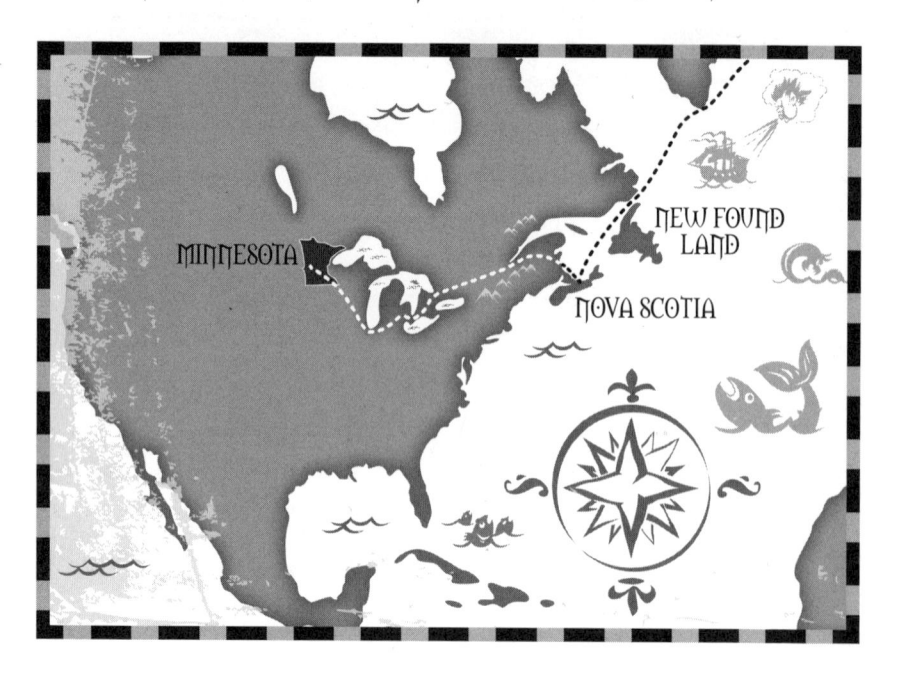

Dearest Hildy,

(I know you hate it when I call you that. I just want to tease you in writing since I'm not there to taunt you in person verbally!)

It was so good to have Uncle Gustav welcome us personally as we landed in Nova Scotia. He'd arranged a cozy room for us with feather beds. I had not slept well throughout the voyage in the rugged accommodations. I wasted no time sinking into the comfort of that fluffy heaven for some catch-up sleep. Not Ole. He went off with Thorvald to explore some of the local sites.

Thorvald had visited Halifax many times and with each visit, learned more about its early history. He was willing to share his knowledge with Ole who was an eager listener and learner.

They went first to meet the sakmaw, chief of the native Mi'Kmaq Indians. Thorvald and Ole were greeted warmly with the friendliness of one who lives up to a name that means "my friends" and is pronounced "Mik-mak."

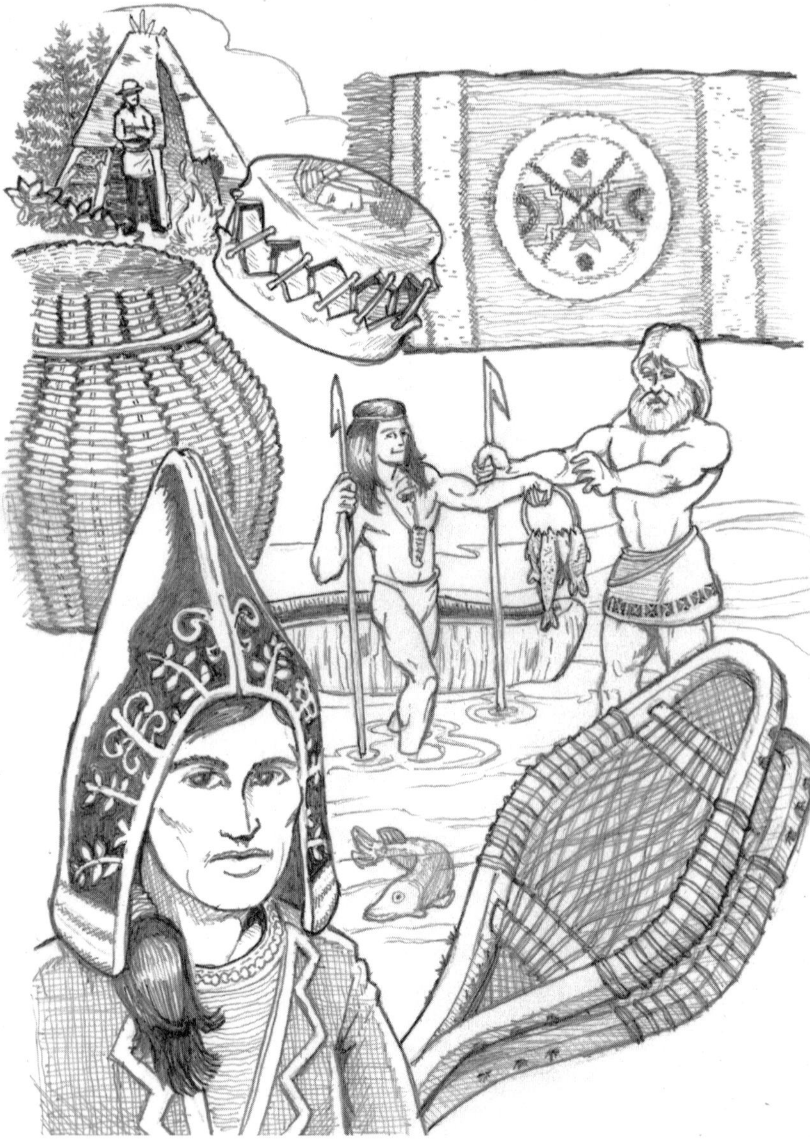

The sakmaw told stories of building wigwams made of spruce logs covered with birch bark layered like shingles. He told how they hunt moose, first injuring them with an arrow to slow them down, then sending their hungry dogs to chase them toward home where the kill was finished with spears.

They did this to have the moose fall nearer to their wigwams so the women, who were in charge of butchering, would not have to drag them so far to dress them out.

Ole only half-heartedly listened to the stories the old Indian man told. He was more interested in the Mik-mak spearheads made from bone, as compared to his which was chiseled from stone.

The conversation shifted and before the two men left the wigwam, Ole had agreed to show the chief how to make a stone spearhead in one easy lesson.

Your loving sister, Mektild

On the Move Again

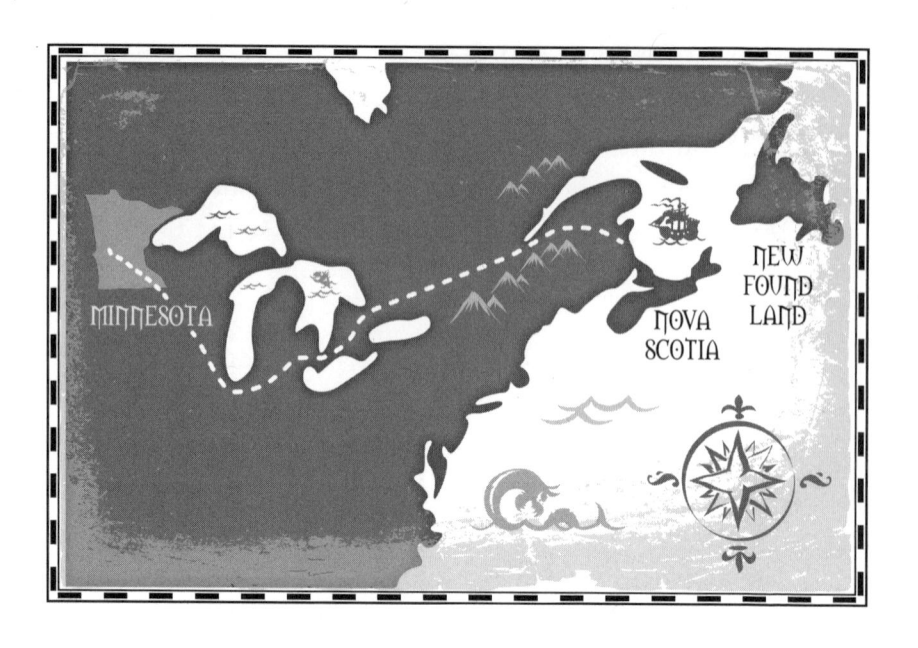

Dearest Sister,

Our stay in Nova Scotia stretched longer than we'd planned. It turned out to be a benefit because we were so exhausted from the long sea voyage and the rest did us good.

When our departure day finally arrived, Ole was to meet us at the train station after his last visit with the sakmaw. True to his spontaneous nature, Ole waited until the last minute to give him the spearhead-making lesson. Uncle Gustav took me to the train station in his one-hitch wagon and Ole was nowhere in sight. I was afraid I would have to leave without him and hope Uncle Gustav would help him find his own way westward!

I waited on the platform until I heard the final "All Aboard!" whistle, tearful that I might have to leave Ole behind.

The train began to inch its way from the station when suddenly, a tribe of Mik-mak Indians with feathered headbands galloped up on horseback.

From their midst, my little Ole, feathers streaming

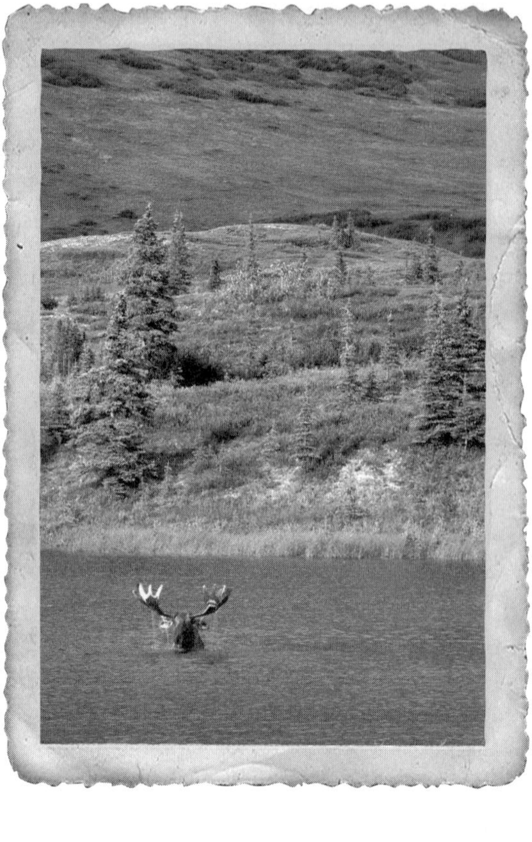

behind him, made one giant leap for a perfect landing on the rear platform of the moving train!

In that moment, I knew Ole was destined for exciting adventures and tried not to think of the dangers he could be facing with his risky behavior.

As I write this letter, we are winding our way through a countryside that looks so much like Norden it makes me a little homesick.

The slopes along the beautiful Bay of Fundy are not as steep as the fjords of home, nor are the rivers as deep.

Some areas of the jagged coastline provide good harbors and rich fishing grounds for the locals, I'm told.

We anticipate much more scenic beauty as we follow the maritime lands into Canada on our way to Detroit which is in America. I am grateful we have made it this far in good health and without any disaster befalling us.

Hoping this finds you and all the family in good health.

With love to all, Mektild

Letters from Big Ole's Mother

Chapter Five

On American Soil

My Dear Sister Bornhild,

The distance between us lengthens as the train continues westward and the days pass, so I'm hoping these letters keep us close in each other's thoughts. Our adventures never cease especially with Ole nearby. Pray tell me, how can anyone be such a hero one minute and the cause of such frustration the next?

While changing trains in Detroit, we heard the screams of a little girl. Ole rushed over and saw a rag doll laying on the railroad track.

Totally unafraid of the oncoming engine, he rushed onto the rails and grabbed the doll out of harm's way. He returned it to the little girl and got a great big smile and a thank-you hug from her. His act of kindness filled me with pride and made him a hero in the eyes of that little girl and her mother.

On our way to Chicago, Ole and I talked about what we could do there during the long time in between trains. We wanted to see the famous water tower that survived the city's horrible fire

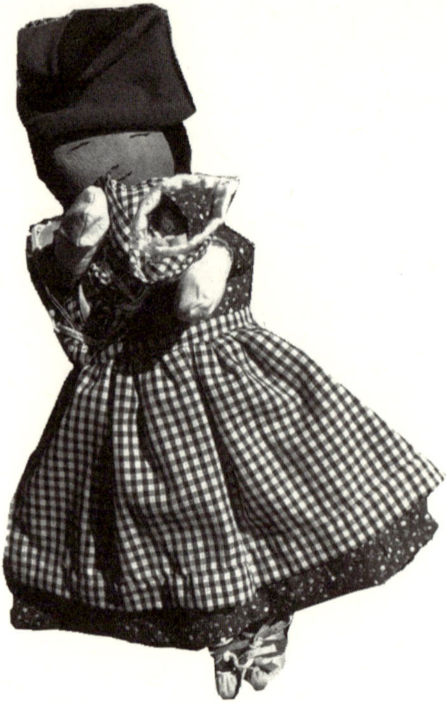

a few years back, and maybe even some of the new buildings. Anything else would depend on finding someone who spoke our language and knew their way around and had transportation for us.

As Ole and I were discussing the possibilities for sightseeing in Chicago, the mother of the little girl whose doll Ole had saved came over to thank him again for his good deed. In gratitude, she invited us to attend the Chicago Black Stockings baseball game with her and her family at Wheeghan Field! Ole's eyes lit up at the thought of seeing this American game that we heard was similar to the game of rounders in our country.

I declined the invitation saying I really needed to rest so Ole went to the baseball game and we agreed to meet later on the next train. I watched Ole walk toward the ballpark knowing he would have plenty to talk about on the long train ride to St. Paul.

Your loving, and tired, sister, Mektild

Wrong Train

Dearest Sister,

A quiet afternoon near the shore of Lake Michigan in Chicago revived me for the short walk back to the train station. I boarded our assigned car to await Ole's return from the baseball game. It was fun to watch everyone board with their shopping bags, balloons, new bonnets, and snack foods they'd acquired during the layover. I watched every person. Each one. No Ole though! I waited anxiously. The train began to move. Still no Ole!

As the train picked up speed and was about to leave the covered bay, I looked through my window into the train next to us. THERE WAS OLE!!! HE WAS ON THE WRONG TRAIN!

Several of the crew heard my cries of anguish and rushed to me. They quickly assured me that the Janesville telegraph operator could alert all

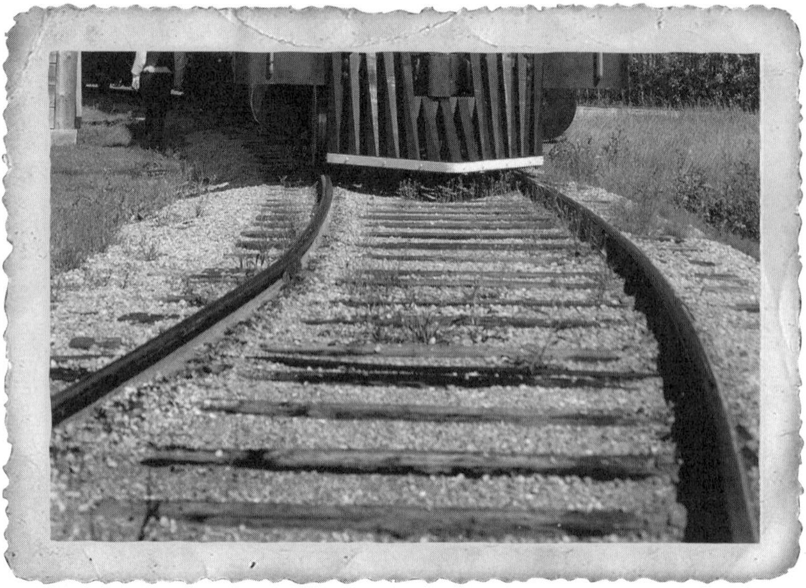

stations along the way to find Ole on the Duluth train and tell him he must change trains at Madison.

I had several more anxious hours until the Lake Geneva depot agent confirmed that Ole had received the message and would join me soon on the right train.

Love from your sister "Tildy"

A Work Stop

Dearest Hildy,

Good news and bad news awaited us at Madison. The good news was to see Ole again. He'd had no trouble traveling alone on the other train and learned more about the Wisconsin state that we were traveling through. He met some families who said they, too, were going to the same area of Minnesota as we were after they visited relatives up on Lake Superior.

The bad news was that heavy rains had washed away the train tracks and left a big sinkhole outside of town near Madison. Crews were working around the clock to do repairs and we got word that more help was needed. They were even seeking volunteers from among the train passengers.

Well, you can already guess who was the first to scramble into the volunteer line, can't you? Yes, your nephew Ole! The recruiters didn't ask his age, his size and muscles spoke for themselves. And since the volunteers would be doing mostly

74

shovel work, he was perfect for that. And experienced!

    They looked to me for a nod of permission. I'm sure Ole was afraid I wouldn't let him go because of the perceived danger. I wanted him to have the opportunity to interact with hard workers and to help others.

    So off he went to become a railroad repair worker.

                      Your loving, and getting older
                            by the day, sister, Mektild

A Hero Again

Dear Bornhild,

   While Ole was helping with the repairs to the railroad track washout near Madison, Wisconsin, he saw two well-dressed men in business suits very close to the edge of the sinkhole. They seemed to be some sort of dignitaries, not common laborers.

   With all the commotion of moving track and ties, plus the digging and the continuing water run-off due to the heavy rains, a sudden gush of water engulfed both the men. One of them toppled over the edge of the hole's embankment and he began to tumble down the slope.

   Ole was the closest to them and he was able to push one man out of the way of the collapse and the other went over the edge and was being swept toward the bottom and deep water. Ole scrambled down the mucky slope and pulled the man to safety! A larger man or fully-grown boy would have been

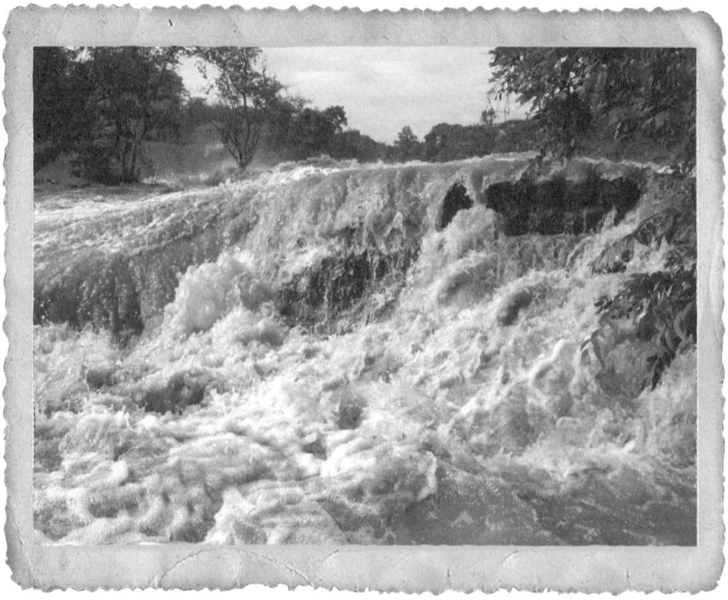

too heavy and the momentum would have taken them both into the water-filled pit.

He was small enough yet strong enough to be able to navigate through the mud without sinking too deeply and pull the man from certain drowning.

Ole's act of courage and quick thinking filled me with pride and made him a hero for the second time on our journey.

It will be good to have a few days layover in St. Paul before continuing to our final destination in Minnesota.

Forever your loving sister and friend, Mektild

Twelve More "Factids" about Big Ole

– Factid #25 –
Big Ole's favorite foods were venison, pan-fried fish, roast turkey and any other wild fowl, potatoes, carrots, turnips and any dessert or baked goods made by his mother.

– Factid #26 –
He never lost an arm wrestling match.

– Factid #27 –
He never spoke a curse word aloud.

– Factid #28 –
He was a talented and skilled cartographer.

– Factid #29 –
He was a good storyteller and loved a good joke.

– Factid #30 –
Big Ole's heritage included a mixture of every Scandinavian genealogy plus some from the Baltic and Germanic peoples.

– Factid #31 –
His mother instilled in him the importance of cultural and ancestral heritage while working toward community progress and personal improvement.

– Factid #32 –
He treasured his Viking longsword that was a family heirloom as well as other cultural artifacts.

– Factid #33 –
His mother downplayed his heroic deeds and accomplishments so he wouldn't become arrogant.

– Factid #34 –
Big Ole loved trains and had aspired to be a locomotive driver and railroad engineer when he was young.

– Factid #35 –
He was talented in handling animals of all kinds although he never owned a domestic pet.

– Factid #36 –
He had perfect teeth and was never ill.

Letters from Big Ole's Mother

Chapter Six

Catching Up

Dear Bornhild,

   We were halfway to St. Paul in Minnesota when Ole finally dredged up the courage to tell me his reason for getting on the wrong train in Chicago.

   He had a great time learning the intricacies of American baseball from the gentlemen who were in the group with him at the game. I realize that what happened was not anyone's fault, not even his. It was not because of some misbehavior or mistake on someone else's part. Still, strange things just seem to happen to Ole wherever he goes.

   Even while experiencing his dream of seeing a professional baseball game, misfortune wasn't far away. He just happened to be sitting where a "foul ball" whacked him on the head and knocked him a little goofy! He seemed fine to those with him and nobody thought he needed medical attention.

   It's a wonder he still had enough wits about him to find a train at all when he was delivered to the station. Even so, he wasn't alert enough to realize there would be more than just one train heading west.

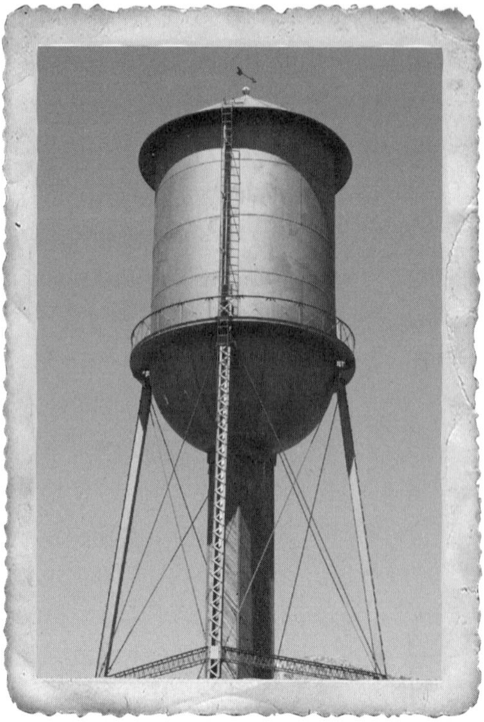

Our previous experience with trains had been only in small towns where just one train came in and you boarded it.

It wasn't until he asked the conductor which car I was in that he became aware of his dilemma. And thank God it was all fairly easily resolved because all the railroad officials were so helpful in getting us reunited before he ended up in Duluth.

Must go – we are making a water stop and I can use some fresh air and walking!

Your loving and travel weary, sister, Tildy

Enjoying the Scenery

Dearest Sister,

With each passing day, I am most grateful for your thoughtful going-away gift of needles and yarn that has allowed me to keep productive and cope better with Ole's ups and downs. I have knitted and purled my way across the miles as I drink in the beauty of the ever-changing scenery. The train has crawled along rivers, around the hills and through pastoral valleys dotted with grazing sheep and cattle.

I have met several other Scandian passengers who have added richness to our journey. They make my days less lonely, especially with Ole usually off somewhere listening to yet another seasoned traveler telling stories that were teaching him things a young boy shouldn't know.

In one conversation with a local traveler, I learned why Wisconsin is called "the badger state." In the early days of lead mining, the miners dug into the hillsides for their shelter, much like a badger does.

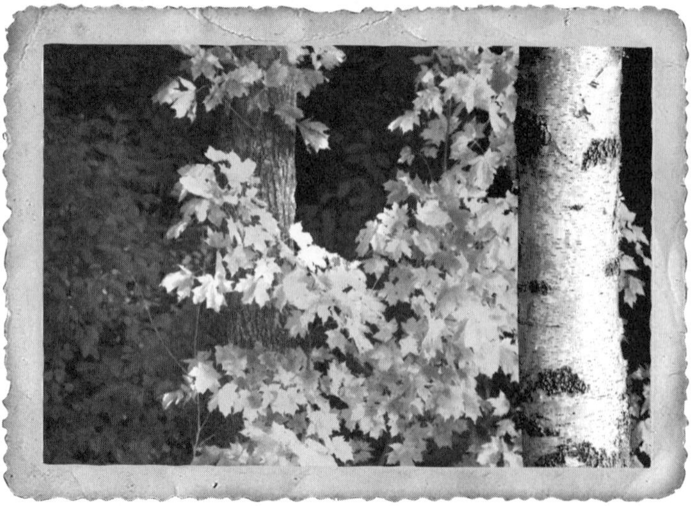

So the miners were nicknamed "badgers" and eventually anyone living in the state of Wisconsin was called that.

As we gaze out our train windows, the landscape flashes by in a kaleidoscope of color. The sun shining down on the granite quarries brings out their brilliant hues. It reminds me of the rocky hills of Norden. I was told that before the discovery of granite in North America, red granite was shipped here by sea from Finland and Sweden. That somehow makes a fine connection between my old world and my new world.

The train is slowing so we must be coming to another stop and I'll have a chance for some fresh air and walking around again.

Until next time, I remain,
your loving sister, Mektild

Letters from Big Ole's Mother

Chapter Seven

Ole's River Plunge

Dearest Hildy,

Ole has become more aware of the world around him and how large our new home really is. He spends much of his time on the train gazing through the windows. He feels a familiar comfort of home whenever we pass a cluster of small lakes or a forest of arborvitae. His greatest thrills have come from things he sees for the first time in America.

Just yesterday he saw an Indian on horseback leaving behind a slow-moving oxcart along a dusty, rutted trail. He was amazed by the hundreds of railroad workers, many of them perhaps our fellow countrymen, laying another westward section of track.

We were both rendered in awe at our first sighting of the mighty Mississippi River. We saw its frothy waters tumbling over the rocks in Minneapolis. We heard its rushing current along the shores in St. Cloud.

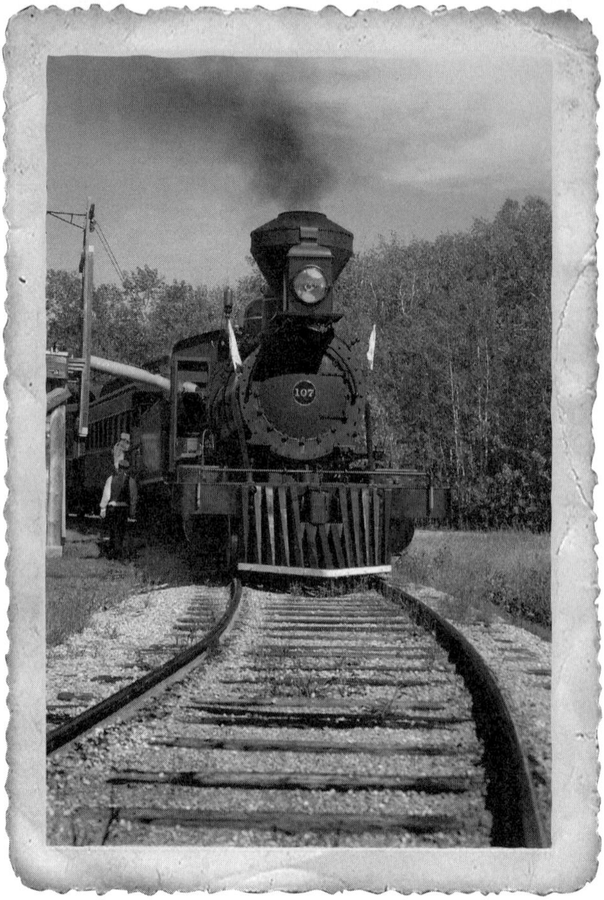

Ole claimed he could hear the voice of the river and longed to plunge right in at its beckoning. The moment our train stopped, Ole scrambled off the car, dashed off the platform and straight to the water's edge. Off came his shoes and socks as he plunged almost in one fluid motion into the icy "Father of Waters." A few seconds was all he needed to create a memory that will stay with him probably for the rest of his life.

Crossing the boundary of the Mississippi River brings us closer to our new home as we wind our way northwest. I'm glad for a day-long layover in St. Cloud. I can do some shopping and it will be good to walk around on firm ground instead of a moving train.

I'll continue another letter as soon as we are back on board because I still have much catching up to do with news.

As ever, your loving sister, Tildy

Brown Beans and a Gold Keepsake

Dearest Sister,

During our layover in St. Cloud, Ole discovered an eatery called Cafe Stuga and was drawn in by the pleasing aroma of what he thought was Brown Beans wafting from inside. We couldn't resist a home country meal and the beans were delicious! Heavily laden with the mingling flavors of onions and spices, served with flatbread, that meal was a back-home treat we'd not had since we left so many weeks ago.

After that wonderful lunch and a nice walk around this small town, Ole was sitting quietly beside me back on board the train. He was so deep in thought, not saying a word, I thought he was asleep. I glanced up from my knitting and saw he was fiddling with a small object, something I'd not seen before.

It gleamed a shiny gold and I couldn't imagine what it was or where he'd gotten it. I feared he might have stolen it since I knew he did not have enough money to buy anything as expensive looking as that. I finally questioned him.

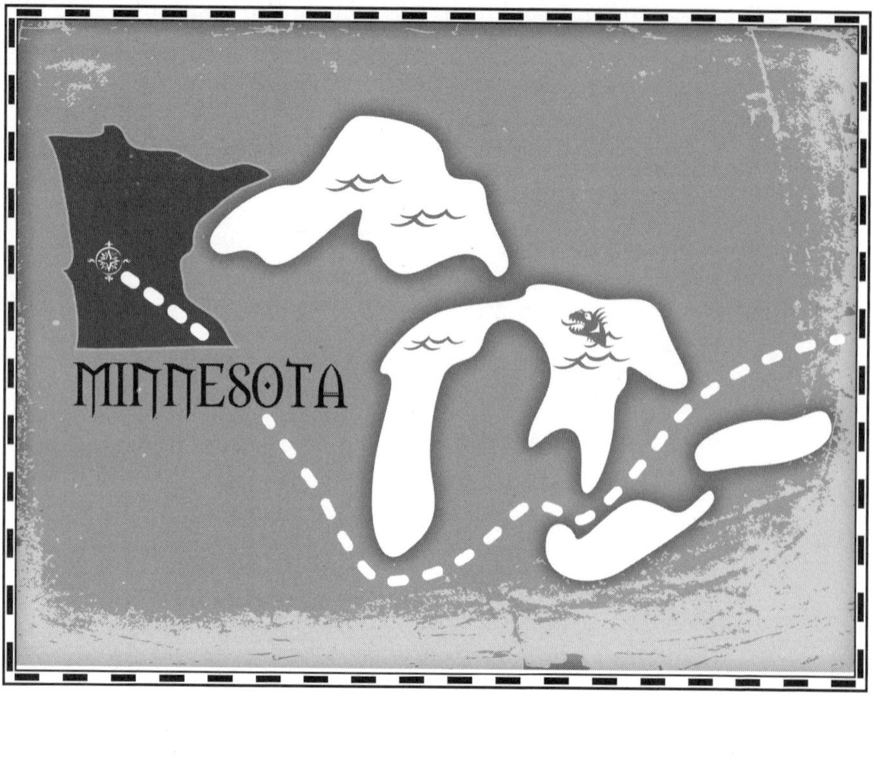
MINNESOTA

He told me it was just a fountain pen he'd found in the mud after rescuing those two men in Madison, Wisconsin. He had picked it up thinking it might belong to one of them. He couldn't find them in the confusion of that mudslide and near-disaster. He had looked for someone official or in authority to give it to and finding none, he just put it in his pocket. If he ever saw them again, he could return it.

It will serve as a reminder of his heroic act in saving two men's lives.

The train is now crossing another river, this one smaller than the Mississippi and full of granite boulders. I think we'll soon be at the final stop of our journey!

Eagerly waiting our destination, Tildy

NEW HOME AT LAST

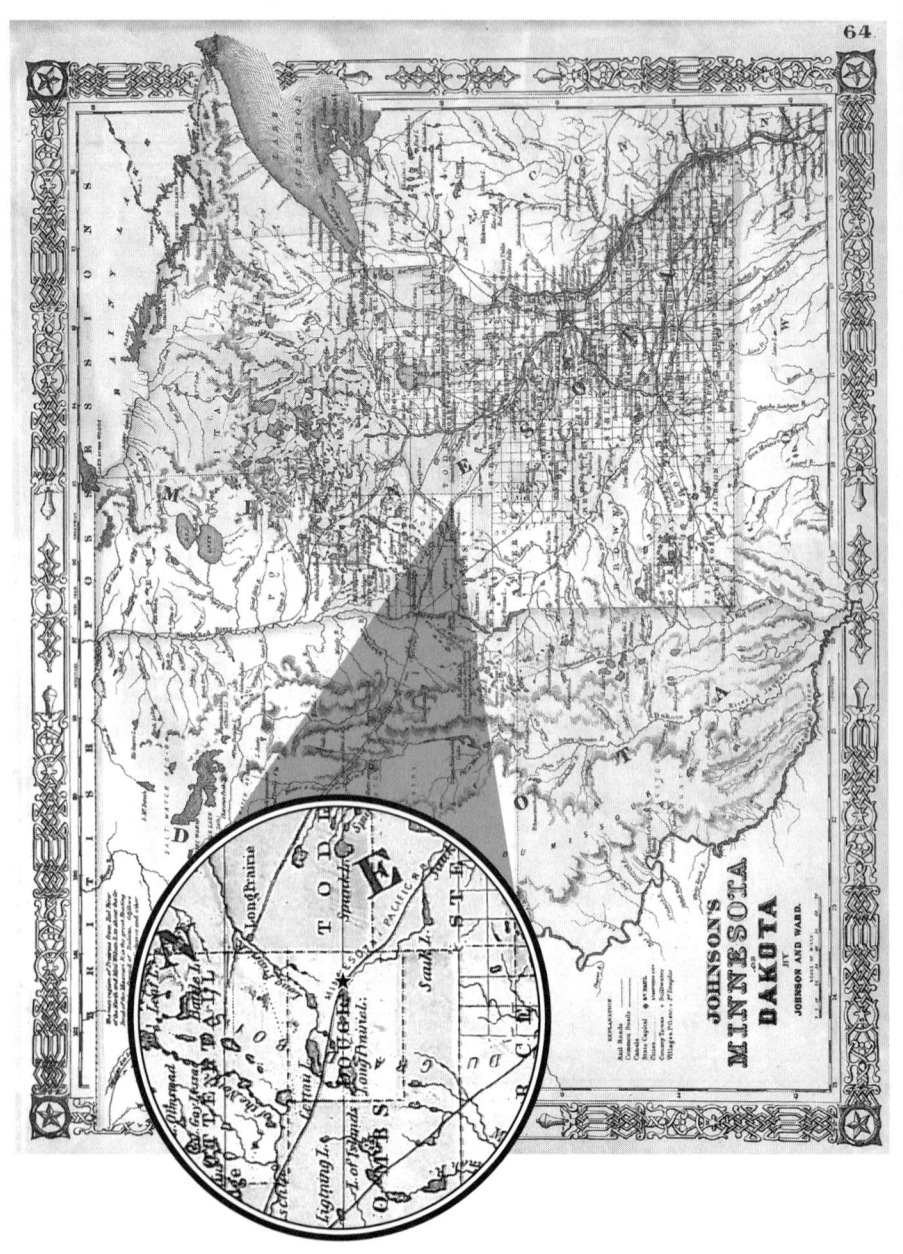

My dear sister, Bornhild,

The train is nearing our destination in Alexandria now. Ole and I will remain seated and let all the initial bustling and milling around subside before disembarking.

Many people are crowding onto the platform and it's a pleasure to see the joy on all their faces, those greeting the passengers and those who are coming to a new home like we are.

Such a crowd! Seems there are at least two or three people to meet each one getting off the train. I don't know how Ole and I will find our cousins, Wilhelm and Aleksander, or how they will find us!

As we were scanning the crowd, waiting our turn to get down from the train, Ole thought he'd caught a glimpse of one of the men he saved back in Madison! Just as quickly, the man disappeared into the crowd. Ole said he would try to find that man on the platform or later in the town.

FORT ALEXANDRIA 1862

AH! The conductor is about to enter our car so we'll be getting off the train soon! This is our final land destination and so begins our new life in America. I couldn't be happier!

I hope Ole doesn't get into trouble here. It will be a big job trying to keep him safe and responsible during his future adventures.

I must continue this later.

        As always, I am your loving sister, Mektild

Ole the Tradesman

Twelve More "Factids" about Big Ole

– Factid #37 –
Big Ole owned many Viking artifacts of his family's collection, some of which featured old runic markings and inscriptions.

– Factid #38 –
He worked as a farm hand and jack-of-all-trades throughout Douglas County, Pope County, Todd County, Ottertail County and many other surrounding areas even crossing borders into the Dakotas, Wisconsin, Iowa, and northward into Canada on occasion.

– Factid #39 –
Big Ole's feet on his statue would be a size 52 extra-wide in today's shoe size measurements.

– Factid #40 –
Big Ole helped build most of the
roads around Alexandria.

– Factid #41 –
He once lost a bet and had to sing a solo at the
opera house in Sauk Centre.

– Factid #42 –
Big Ole helped build the Hotel Alexandria on
Lake Geneva in 1883.

– Factid #43 –
He helped design and build many of the
first lake cottages in the Alexandria area
where he honed his skills and helped
supplement his mother's income.

– Factid #44 –
He once won a dance contest in Long Prairie.

– Factid #45 –
He became a skilled pilot for Minnesota's big lake passenger boats and cargo vessels.

– Factid #46 –
Big Ole's first cousin, his mother's sister's daughter, married a Swedish prince.

– Factid #47 –
He organized impromptu baseball teams for fun in Alexandria and helped teach local children, teens, and even adults how to play the game.

– Factid #48 –
His mother, Mektild Valdis Guld, had been born on July 4, 1848 on the same island where she gave birth to Ole. He was born on her birthday in 1867.

Excerpts from Letters
and Journals

Chapter Eight

The letters and journal entries from Mektild after she and Ole arrived in Alexandria were lost or badly damaged.

The remaining fragments which were discovered after the first bundle of letters, provide only a sketchy account of Big Ole's time in Alexandria.

Early Days in Alexandria
(Circa 1882-85)

(Letter Excerpt) Cousins Wilhelm and Aleksander took us to sign some legal papers in the presence of their attorney and friend, Mr. Knute Nelson, a Norwegian who also knew our language.

It was right after Ole's 15th birthday and he was so proud to wear his new suit coat. He had placed that keepsake gold pen into his breast pocket thinking it made him look more grown-up.

That pen was a proud souvenir of rescuing those two men at the railroad cave-in at St. Paul just a couple years back. Ole had attempted to find the owner then.

As soon as we walked into Mr. Nelson's office, he recognized his pen and almost instantly realized it was Ole who had saved his life in Madison, Wisconsin. They struck up a lively conversation reminiscing about that day and they developed a strong friendship.

Mr. Nelson was impressed with Ole's acts of heroism and his eagerness to learn. Ole became a valuable community member with the reputation for being a diligent and skilled worker.

He offered to help Ole meet more people, develop more skills, and learn more about the community. Ole became an apprentice law clerk for Mr. Nelson and got to use the gold pen occasionally for official work.

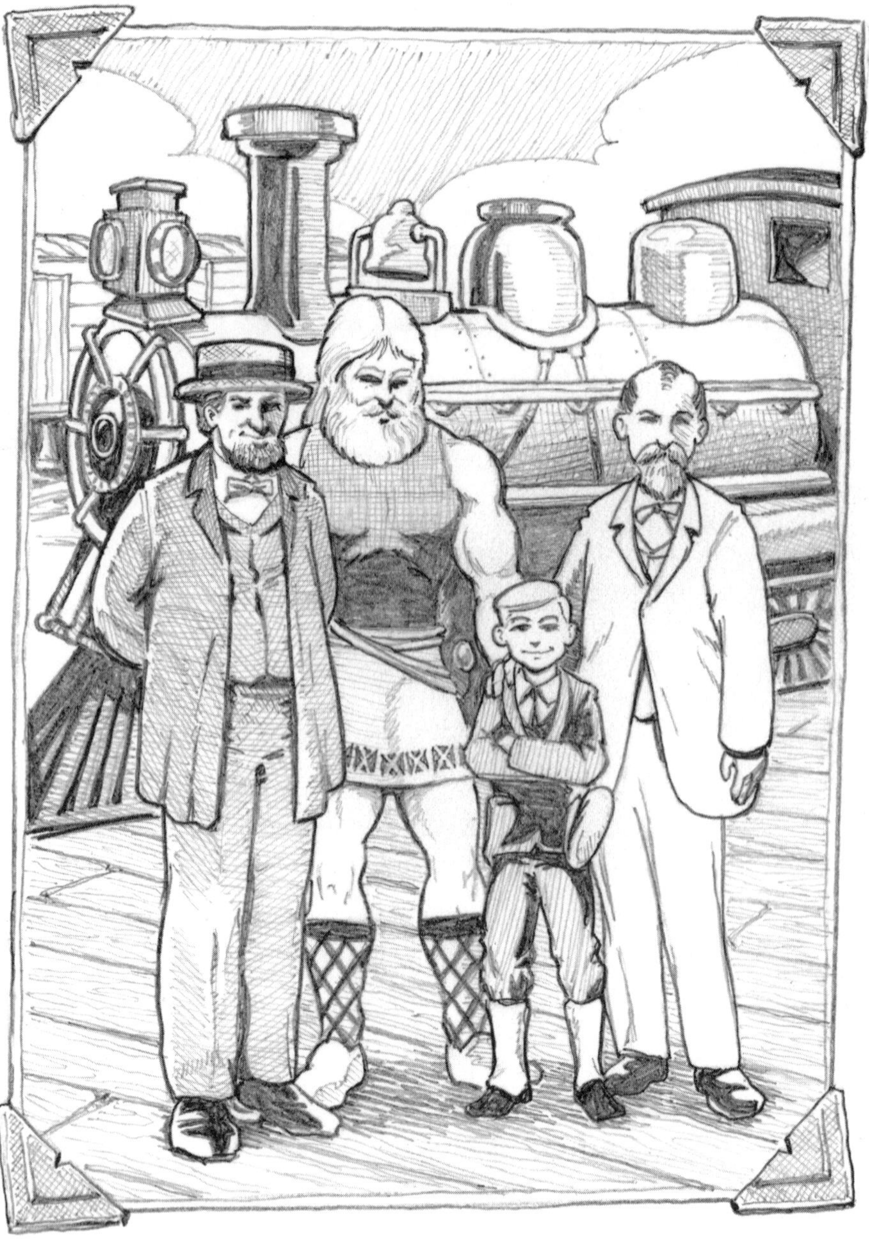

Ole's Formative Years
(Circa 1882-85)

Mr. Nelson inspired Ole to become more educated. He began reading everything he could. He especially liked the books in Mr. Nelson's private collection. Several other townspeople had started a lending library and Ole made good use of that private service. He made new friends throughout his self-educational pursuits.

Ole attracted people through his friendliness and willingness to help others. His natural charm, rugged good looks, and the intelligence gave him the demeanor of a statesman.

Mr. Nelson came to regard Ole as the son he never saw grow up. Ole respected Knute Nelson as the father figure he always needed.

Ole found good work with townspeople, including merchants and businessmen, as a handyman. Country folks hired him to help on their farms during different seasons.

He worked hard to learn several trades and skills from picking rock to laying railroad ties, carpentry to blacksmithing. He had learned many useful life skills from his mother while growing up and considered cooking and baking as great hobbies.

A frequent visitor of Mr. Nelson's was his friend James J. Hill, the railroad baron and land developer.

On one occasion, the three were fishing along with Mr. Hill's young son, Louis, when a sudden summer squall raged across the lake. The boat capsized and all were flung into the roiling water.

Ole saw little Louis struggling mightily for his life and out of reach of the other men.

With Ole's strength and agility as a sturdy young man, he was able to swim to the lad and pull him to shore. The other men were fine swimmers and everyone survived the ordeal.

A very grateful Mr. Hill came to regard Ole as part of his family. He placed Ole on his land development and survey team to act as liaison with local farmers, merchants, bankers and politicians.

By this time, Ole had become well educated and knew many people, including local Indians, who regarded him highly as a fine man of integrity, resourcefulness, dependability and competence.

116

Becoming an Important Leader

Ole's prior connections with Indians in Nova Scotia helped him understand the blending of cultures and made him a good prospect to discuss social and economic issues with the Indians and the farmers around Kensington.

During one of his first survey explorations for Mr. Hill, Ole discovered some markings on artifacts found near old mooring stones. One of the inscriptions matched a rune mark on his long-sword that he'd brought from his homeland.

Ole realized then that his ancestors, perhaps even his own absent father might have set foot on this land Ole now called home.

The Marrying Kind

Ole's work ethic and popularity, along with his rugged good looks and affable manner, put him on the social scene as one of the most eligible bachelors in central Minnesota.

Ole found true love when he first laid eyes on Metina, a pretty maiden of "mixed breed." She and Ole shared a commonality: He had been abandoned at a young age by his father and she by her white mother who had been unable to assimilate into the Ojibwe culture.

They met during the Maple Sugar Moon, the third moon according to an ancient Anishanabe belief. They married during the Moose-Calling Moon, the Ninth Moon, which was a Mi'Kmaq tradition and a way of honoring his first friendship with Native peoples upon first landing in North America. They received blessings from relatives and friends on all sides of their multi-cultural families.

Untimely Death of a Hero

Ole continued his calling as a community leader while also working for the livery and dray services as a transportation supervisor. His duties involved scheduling the delivery of passengers and baggage to the hotels and resorts.

One evening when many dignitaries and politicians were in town to open new businesses and public buildings, Ole had to fill in as a driver.

Following a social event, he was driving his mother and his wife back home. As they were crossing the railroad tracks, an axle snapped, stranding the rig on the rails.

Ole managed to get his wife and mother to safety and started back for the horses and wagon. The horses spooked and reared up at the sound of an oncoming train.

Ole slipped on the icy rail and was knocked unconscious on the tracks, just seconds before the oncoming locomotive hit.

His final act of heroism saved his mother, his wife, and unbeknownst to him, his unborn child.

Metina was going to break this good news about her pregnancy to Ole later that evening when they were back home.

Ole's courage and strength saved his family and his offspring. Like his father, Ole would not be there to see his child grow up to carry on the family heritage and keep alive the legacy of his ancestors.

During Ole's funeral service attended by hundreds of people from all over the region, Mr. Knute Nelson, Mr. James J. Hill and many state officials and leaders spoke of his greatness.

One dignitary commented, "**Some day, this community will create a monument, an enormous statue, honoring the man who so aptly represents the spirit and true meaning of the establishment of this great country.**"

Big Ole died on November 4, 1899
in Alexandria, Minnesota,
United States of America.

EPILOGUE

Big Ole's mother, Mektild, lived to age 85. She supported herself throughout her entire life. After Big Ole's untimely death, she stayed with her daughter-in-law and grandson. She worked the rest of her life on small farms and rural properties acquired through Big Ole in several areas of Pope County, Douglas County, Todd County, and Ottertail County.

Big Ole's wife, Metina, had been a bride just eight months when she was widowed. She never remarried. Big Ole's son, also named Ole, coincidentally was born on July 4, 1900, sharing the same birthday as his father and his grandmother.

The two women worked together and raised Ole Jr. without a father, just as Big Ole had been raised.

In the next generation, Mektild saw the birth of her great-grandchild, Big Ole's granddaughter, Big Ole Jr.'s daughter, Marlina Maginhilde (nicknamed Margie). She was born in 1923 and was 10 years old when Mektild died in 1933.

Twelve More "Factids" about Big Ole

– Factid #49 –
Big Ole had intricate skills as a blacksmith. He helped make most of the nails and some of the iron-work for the finishing hardware for many buildings downtown and in residences during the mid-1880s and 1890s.

– Factid #50 –
In his 20s, Big Ole was the most eligible bachelor in the entire mid-section of Minnesota.

– Factid #51 –
He held a patent on a farm implement improvement and donated the profits to the local schools.

– Factid #52 –
Big Ole assisted in brokering peace between white settlers and Native Americans near Breckenridge and Fergus Falls.

– Factid #53 –
He was an apprentice law clerk in his early days in Alexandria.

− Factid #54 −
He made his own ceremonial Viking costumes based on ancient drawings which he wore at state and local events for entertainment and educational purposes.

− Factid #55 −
He died before seeing the birth of his only child.

− Factid #56 −
Big Ole's true surname remains a mystery. It is known that his lineage includes the names Akesson, Ericson, Gustafson, Olson, Swanson and Svenson.

− Factid #57 −
His burial site was kept a secret by his wife and is believed to be on land dedicated to Native Americans.

− Factid #58 −
His statue depiction in Alexandria was built in 1964 and sent to New York to be on display at the World's Fair in 1965.

− Factid #59 −
The Big Ole statue in Alexandria is the cover photo on a book titled "Oddball Minnesota" by Jerome Pohlen.

− Factid #60 −
The Big Ole statue in Alexandria, Minnesota, stands 28-feet tall, weighs 4 tons.

Big Ole Statue Location
Big Ole Central Park, on the south shore of Lake Agnes near the intersection of Broadway and 2nd Ave. in Alexandria, Minnesota.

Minnesota Statuary

Statues depicting legendary big guys in Minnesota include Pierre the Voyageur at Two Harbors, Chief Wenonga at Battle Lake, Chief Moose Dung (no, we're not kidding!) at Thief River Falls and Paul Bunyan in several locations including Bemidji and Brainerd.

The alleged burial site of Paul Bunyan in Kelliher proclaims he lived from 1794 to 1899 which would make him 105 years old at the time of his demise.

One of the few statues of women that aren't generic representations of real pioneers or modern TV stars is Paul Bunyan's girlfriend (or wife, if you believe the contrived marriage certificate) in Hackensack. She's Lucette Diana Kensack (1952) and is 17ft. tall.

Gnomes and trolls make steady appearances (one is a beer-drinking troll) as do many saints and immigrants, even a god: Thor, the Viking God of Thunder.

Imaginary creatures include sea serpents, mermaids, iron man, Uncle Sam, Happy Chef, Statue of Liberty, and the entire cast of Peanuts cartoon characters. The world's largest stucco snowman resides in St. Paul.

Military heroes are abundant in many parks. Sports heroes adorn athletic fields and college campuses.

Water towers provide a sort of statuary and are dressed up or disguised as a fish bobber, an ear of corn, hot air balloon and a teapot. Some water towers have scenic views painted on them.

Some of the oddities depicted in Minnesota statuary include a doorknob, giant clothespin, cup of coffee being poured out, a human foot, dinosaur skeletons, and a gigantic spoon and cherry. Perhaps the oddest gigantic piece is an actual ball of twine.

World's Fair Debut

The Big Ole statue first appeared in public at the New York World's Fair for the second half of the 1964-65 two-year event held from April to October each year. He stood proudly amongst other Viking-themed displays in the Minnesota Pavilion along with the actual Kensington Runestone. At least 50 million people were introduced to Big Ole before he traveled back across the country to his home in Alexandria.

The Big Ole Statue has been moved several times within Alexandria and now has its own park, near the original Fort Alexandria, where hundreds of thousands of visitors have taken millions of photographs with the iconic legend. This is a timeline of the statue history:

1964 – The idea for a giant Viking statue was conceived as a second-year addition to the 1964-65 New York World's Fair. Big Ole was chosen as the representative of Minnesota to stand with the Kensington Runestone in the display.

April 1965

The Big Ole statue was completed by sculptor Gordon Schumaker of Gordon Displays in Minneapolis and shipped on a specially designed flatbed trailer to New York for its debut.

December 1965

Big Ole was returned to Alexandria after his tour of duty at the World's Fair and was given a place of honor atop a concrete pedestal in the middle of the traffic intersection on Broadway and 3rd Avenue. He overlooked the downtown facing south, welcoming visitors in a large way.

December 1967

Big Ole was dressed for the holidays in gigantic Santa Claus garb when a prankster shot a flaming arrow into his cape. The resulting severe burns sent Big Ole to trauma care. Repairs were finished at his original manufacturing site, Gordon Displays in Minneapolis.

Big Ole Injury Report

Throughout his lifetime, Big Ole has sustained many wear-and-tear injuries as well as weather-related damage or vandalism. He was knocked off his foundation by a freak wind storm in his early years before he resided in his current park site. His spear got broken in another wind episode. The worst damage occured when he was crushed under a roof collapse at his storage location when he used to be stored inside over the winter. He's been repainted many times throughout his statue life. The decorative wings on his helmet have blown off more than once and needed replacement, the most recent incident taking place in June 2014.

August 1980

The State Department of Transportation declared the Big Ole statue a traffic hazard because he stood where traffic lights were going to be installed. The new location one block north was in front of the Runestone Museum and Chamber of Commerce.

Spring 1985

The Big Ole statue was now 20 years old and needed some structural repairs as well as his first repainting.

Summer and Fall 1996

Big Ole received a newly-repaired sword, a bath, and a repainting with the help of many organizations and businesses. A new parking lot was completed and the wooden steps to the statue were rebuilt.

While he had stood in the intersection on 3rd and Broadway, the constant vibrations of traffic had loosened his underpinnings. Ropes and wires had been placed around his neck and shoulders to steady him and those resulted in some wear and tear.

Even with his new refurbishing, by October 1996 he was still a bit shaky so he was taken down and put into storage to be repaired over the winter. That's when the roof caved in and damaged him further requiring major repairs to be completed.

Spring 1997

Big Ole was welcomed back to his standing place in an "Ole Oppe Fest" as his homecoming party. Amidst all the revelry, the City Council ordered that the Big Ole statue had to be moved from the intersection.

An increasing number of visitors wanted their photo taken with the big statue. It was becoming a safety issue for the pedestrians who had to cross traffic for their photo opportunity next to Big Ole.

Summer 2007

Big Ole found a new home across the street from Fort Alexandria along the Central Lakes Trail in Big Ole Park where he stands today in a very appropriate spot that's safer for pedestrians to park and climb the platform for a photo opportunity with Big Ole.

2012-2013

Big Ole Park has seen continuing improvements to the grounds by several community organizations. These include public art, a colorful metal sculpture and benches, a meditation garden across the street with flowers and a gazebo, additional parking spaces, new home of the Farmer's Market, and long kiosk displaying history and trail information.

November 2013

The Big Ole statue is featured on the Runestone Museum's collector Christmas ornament series reinstituted after a five-year lapse.

Summer 2014

The Ole Oppe Fest returned on Memorial Day Weekend with a big celebration at The Fort. Private funding continues to support the upkeep of Big Ole's statue.

Minnesota "Big People" Statue Comparisons

Big Ole in Alexandria (1965)
Height: 28 ft., standing
Weight: 8,000 lb.

Jolly Green Giant in Blue Earth (1978)
Height: 55 ft., standing
Weight: 8,000 lb

Paul Bunyan in Akeley (1984)
Height: 28 ft., kneeling on one knee
(50 ft. if he were standing)
Weight: not known

Paul Bunyan in Bemidji (1937)
Height: 18 ft., with Babe the Blue Ox, 10 ft tall
Weight: unknown

Paul Bunyan in Brainerd (1949)
Height: 26 ft., seated
Weight: 5,000 lb.

Smokey Bear in International Falls (1953)
Height: 26 ft., standing
Weight: not known

"Quest" the Viking in Spring Grove (Yr. not known)
Height: 15 ft., standing
Weight: unknown

Hermann the German in New Ulm (1940)
Height: 32 ft., standing; total with base: 102 ft.
Weight: 4,400 lb.

Big Ole's Mother
MEKTILD VALDIS GULD
ᛘᛖᚲᛏᛁᛚᛞ ᛈᚨᛚᛞᛁᛋ ᚷᚢᛚᛞ

Big Ole's mother lives in the imagination of writer Marjorie Van Gorp, a descendent of Scandinavian immigrants. The character of Mektild is inspired by her maternal grandmother, Minnie Fischer. The journey itself is based on emigration of her father, Carl Engstrand, from Sweden to Spruce Hill, Douglas County, Minnesota, in 1893.

The Legend Creators

Marjorie Engstrand Joslyn Van Gorp has a proud lineage that includes Swedish immigrants who settled the northeast corner of Douglas County, Minnesota, working the rich farmland of Spruce Hill Township. She was the youngest child of Carl and Hattie Fischer Engstrand of Rose City, born on June 19, 1923. She learned early to stand strong and fight for rightful attention in a family of four siblings who were all just a year apart.

Her passion for knowledge was instilled by her father and she developed a deep respect for education and lifelong learning.

At a time when an 8th grade education was considered satisfactory for a woman to have a successful life, Marge wanted more. So at age 14, she was allowed to leave home and attend high school in Alexandria. She lived with families and helped with the children and household chores in exchange for room and board.

She became a wartime bride and military wife within a year after high school graduation while seeking adventure that began in California. She lived in Texas, Alaska, Nebraska, North Dakota, Florida, and in the Azores, Portugal.

Widowed at age 45, Marge began a new chapter in her life back home again in Alexandria where she worked as a copywriter for a radio station and then as a travel agent. She visited all of the states in the U.S. as well as many island nations in the Caribbean, all the countries of Scandinavia, and nearly all the countries in Europe. She enjoyed trips to South America and Singapore.

Another new adventure began when she met her second husband. Their blind date began as a two-hour conversation over dinner that led to a 20-year romance that didn't end until his death in 1998.

One year after being widowed for the second time, Marge returned to Alexandria.

No matter where she'd lived or traveled, her love of learning and accomplishing new things never waned. She'd gone back to school at age 40 to become a beautician and supplement family income. At age 50, a renewed interest in writing prompted her to enroll in professional classes.

Marge always loved to write. Her first writing experience was for the *Alex High Times* during her high school years from 1937-41. She gathered more expertise as a writer for military base newspapers and radio. She wrote scripts for her own radio show as an on-air personality. She joined writers clubs, Toastmasters, and other organizations for the opportunity to explore different kinds of writing such as publicity, reports, advertising and journalism.

Her interests spanned a wide variety of hobbies that showcased her talents. Marge took a quilting class when she was 60, followed by oil painting classes. She became quite adept in both those art forms and received awards on her work. When she was 70, she took a bookbinding class.

Marge became interested in genealogy in the mid-1980s when she started tracing her own family history and became a researcher at the Douglas County Historical Society.

In 1991, Marge became a self-published book author with *Tapestries* featuring her original poetry, an art form she began in elementary school.

When she was in her early 80s, she got more serious about improving her writing and editing skills so enrolled in college classes. She completed two courses at Alexandria Technical and Community College and attended several professional writing workshops.

In 2003, Marge began penning a four-part series, the *Spruce Hill Anthology* while serving on the Historic Spruce Hill Church board. Her interest in history and writing skills landed her the job of columnist for a local newspaper.

In 2008, she was recruited as a contributing editor and writer for *Definitive Woman Magazine* joining a staff and list of freelance writers whose ages ranged from 20 to her own 85 years.

She keeps learning and keeps accomplishing and says that's been one of her keys to vitality and longevity. She has a daughter and a son who have given her a line of descendants that include grandchildren, great-grandchildren, and great-great-grandchildren.

She's still blazing trails and knocking down a few brick walls of personal obstacles along the way. She's always been able to redefine and rebuild at every stage in her life and that pattern continues now into her 9th decade of purposeful living.

Julie Zuehlke retired from teaching mass communication and public relations as a college professor and went back into journalism. She's the editor of *Definitive Woman Magazine* in Alexandria. Her other publishing credits include newspapers, magazines, books and scholarly work. She operates her private business service in integrated marketing communications, organizational development and strategic planning. Julie volunteers with several organizations in the community and seves on boards of directors.

Kerry Olson shares her artistic talents as an advertising consultant and graphic designer in her own business, KO Creative. She brings more than 20 years experience in marketing, brand imaging, and product development to her work. She's served a national clientele in advertising agency affiliation, does commission paintings, and currently is co-publisher and director of creative for *Definitive Woman Magazine*, published by AMP-Squared.

ORDERING INFORMATION:

ISBN: 978-0-9897926-0-8

AMP-Squared Books - A Division of AMP2, LLC
316 N. Nokomis Street, Ste. #1, Alexandria MN 56308
(320)763-3742 • Email: books@ampsquared.com
www.ampsquared.com